i

Between Mountain
and River

Thomas F. Sheehan

Pocol Press

Fairfax, VA

POCOL PRESS
Published in the United States of America
by Pocol Press
3911 Prosperity Avenue
Fairfax, VA 22031
www.pocolpress.com

© 2018 by Thomas F. Sheehan

All rights reserved. No part of this book may be reproduced in any form whatsoever without the express written consent of Pocol Press. Exceptions are made for brief quotations for criticism and reviews.

Publisher's Cataloguing-in-Publication

Names: Sheehan, Thomas F., 1928-, author.
Title: Between mountain and river / Thomas F. Sheehan
Description: Clifton, VA: Pocol Press, 2018.
Identifiers: ISBN 978-1-929763-83-2 | LCCN 2018949378
Subjects: LCSH Frontier and pioneer life--West (U.S.)--Fiction. | Cowboys--Fiction. | West (U.S.)--Fiction. | Short stories, American. | Western stories. | Historical fiction. | BISAC FICTION / Westerns | FICTION / Short Stories (single author).
Classification: LCC PS3569.H39216 B48 2018 | DDC 813.6--dc23

Library of Congress Control Number: 2018949378

ACKNOWLEDGEMENTS

Tom Sheehan's stories have appeared in *Rope and Wire Western Lifestyle Magazine*, *Western Online,* and *Literally Stories.*

TABLE OF CONTENTS

Jeremy Slade's Trip to Oblivion	1
Josiah Weaverlake and the Dog Pack	9
Last Stage from Crow's Hill	13
Linked	17
Kid Bullet and the Gainful Ministry	24
Linda Dove's Look-a-like	33
Amigo Juan's War	40
The Horseman of the Davidos	48
Yuma Tranquility	55
Me and Tozzer	61
One Way to McAlister's, or Manitou's Tipi	65
Jehrico and the Cock-Eyed Burro	75
Jehrico's Sign	78
Chase Holman's Kidnapping	83
A Dragoon's Adventure	92
A Garden of Plenty	98
Breakheart Station Master	101
Bounty for a Sheriff	107
Colum Twyne's Last Leg Up	113
A Prairie Christmas Wish	118
Destination Idaho	123

Jeremy Slade's Trip to Oblivion

Never had the search for his father seemed so impossible, so calamitous. It was supposed to be a long search, he always believed, but also a fruitful one full of contemplation of what the end would be like, his getting hugged for the first time in more than a dozen years by a soldier missing since the great war a dozen years earlier. Many times he felt that hug, the power of a loving squeeze, the worldly smell of a man surrounding him and his joy.

It would be worth it all.

But now!

The noise came first, he always said afterward, before his feet felt the rumble in the earth. Before the rumble there was a concussion in the air that came ear-splitting without the sound, all of it warning him the earth was in an uproar and he was on the perilous side of Cougar Mountain just above the river junction. The town was situated downhill at the junction, a new town born of the times and a situation by the river. Suddenly his horse, in one sideways failing, left him, and slid downhill in the mix of rock and boulders into the gray, dusty morning. Cries of his long-time mount ripped at young Slade's soul. With steeled hands the young man grabbed a shelf of rock, the rim of it, hoping the shelf would hold itself in place. The world, to his mind, was in revolt, and this edge of rock was the only thing in the world he had to grab onto.

The rumble continued, a roar growing as if from the center of Earth itself, accompanied by higher pitched shrieks of tearing rocks, and occasional trees tossed as easy as the twigs flying by him on their downward plunge. In the midst of calamity he was, death an almost sure ending to the upheaval, and with it the eternal loss of his father, now lost to all time.

It was so unfair after all he had been through.

In his desperate grip he had wrangled onto a long, broad and thick chunk of mountain ledge. Strata of odd colors graced the face of the rock. He saw red and blue layers or tiers laced into its formation. Now, as it too began to slide, he hoped he could ride it safely downhill. Perhaps other rocks on the fly would not hit him. Perhaps they would. It was his only out, riding it like a sled off the side of the hill or mountain or whatever chunk of earth on which he was hitching his way. He remembered an old timer telling him how he had ridden a snowy avalanche clear to salvation. "I rode the crest of that big boy down to the foot of the damned mountain itself, like I was on skis."

Young Slade, 16 by a matter of days, bound for the town down below to seek out his real father, let his prayers be heard, almost above the storm. "Let me find my pa and let me be happy with him, please,

Lord. That old timer said he might be the lucky one got to here. That's all I ever wanted, to find my pa. I have come so far, ridden so hard, and worked like a fool on an errand."

In a shredded moment of sights and images and figures, his whole life spun through its orbit; he saw it all again, even as the roar and the rumble and the revolution of the earth continued its threat to his journey, to his young life.

Never sure, he believed he could remember his father riding away to battle, his uniform stark blue against the paler sky, his horse a gallant red stallion that loomed over the child as large as a cloud, shaking off the sun, throwing a shadow on the ground. Again, he heard his mother crying that time, saw her tears. Never before had he seen her cry; and he never saw her cry again, she went in such a hurry. Such sights never left him, and he found them anew even as Earth tossed itself into a mad violence.

The partial images, though, just as now, came back often: his father off to the war, his mother just wasting away in a matter of a few years, his paternal grandmother taking him by the hand and walking away from the burial on the side of a hill in Tennessee. That night he had a new bed, a new roof over his head, a new hand scrubbing him in the morning, folding his hands in prayer at night.

Jeremy Slade, on the side of that Blue Ridge Mountain in Tennessee, grew strong, loyal, with a sense of belonging to the Earth itself because he knew many of its parts. He knew the food chain from the roots up, how to survive, how to behave as a man in the face of odds, natural and otherwise. One day, he was sure, the shadow that his father's horse had thrown over him on the day of departure would part, and he would find his father in that full exposure. All reports said the officer was lost in battle near the very end of the war, at West Point, Georgia, on April 16, 1865, near the end of many things known to many people.

One message, years after the battle at West Point, said his father, seriously wounded, had been carried off on a wagon by some local folks. A drummer had come into the valley below the Slade homestead saying that Captain Jeremy Slade had survived the battle and had been taken to a private home near West Point. That news rippled through the valleys of the Blue Ridge and made its way to young Jeremy Slade. When he was 14 he made a trip by himself to find that home, and the family that had cared for his father.

One old man, bushy, dry at the throat, sitting on cabin stoop, told him, after some cajoling and a jug of spirits, "The whole brood of them headed west, 'bout '67, and I heard that one wounded man they took in during the war was with them, still ailing I ain't got an idea of what. But he wasn't the only one they took in. There was other wounded men these docile people took to their bosom. They was Quakers to the core. I never knew any of the soldiers' names, what rank they was, what uniform they chose, for them folks burnt it soon as he got undressed of it."

The old timer, sipping on the given jug, eventually scratched his mind for any word of the family. "They had sons left here back in '58 or '59, before the war, and was headed with the family for a town in Utah called, and I ain't sure of it, but it did sound of hell, a place called Oblivion. That's all I know, son. Oblivion. I'm pretty sure that's the name. And them folks was the Murchins, every last one of them."

Oblivion came up awfully fast, rising from the river junction where two streams converged, like a pair of bridle reins in a fist. It was a new town, breathing like a new-born, coming into its own, and here came Jeremy Slade, out of the mountain range and down into the heart of Oblivion itself. He was a mere mile from the heart of the town, from the saloon, and was saved and thirsty. He could taste the first beer, the only way the desert or fear can appease themselves, by drowning a drink at a time.

That's when the whole Earth began shaking.

The great chunk of ledge, as much a sled or a ski, rode the tumult and the calamity to the ground. At the abrupt end of its journey, it stabbed the earth and shook young Slade loose. He fell at the base of the ledge as it buried a massive portion of itself into the ground and halted its journey well short of Oblivion. It would, in the end, stand upright, possibly immovable for centuries.

Jeremy Slade, alive though skittish for a bit, walked into Oblivion looking for the livery, the hotel, the saloon, and the first person promising familiarity with the town. The saloon came first, his throat dry as ever, his hands frozen yet in the grip he had exercised on his impossible ride. Two ladies, in choice clothing, walked past the general store staring at him. Then the saloon seemed merged at the hip with the store. A young boy, no older than 6 or 7, yelled loudly as he pushed a hoop in the road. He wore knickers with red suspenders, but was shoeless. A man in a battered hat sat whittling at the corner of the general store's porch, his knife blade catching the sun in small pieces, flashing speedy movements. His hands were quick and he did not look up from his task as Slade walked past him.

Slade's throat was burning and he stepped into the saloon to put out the fire. Behind the counter a broad-smiling man worked the bar and put out his hand in welcome. Yet Slade found something else in the air, an essence or an aura that suffused what he had first sensed in the town, the particular odors of an area, and the identity of a town at first call.

Something known hung in the air.

"I say, son," the barkeep said, "you look like you could use some wet down that throat of yours I'm feeling is on fire. Your face, boy, is red as my pappy's suspenders. What you been up to? I know you're new hereabouts."

A tall, sudsy beer came onto the countertop, as his stare made it appear he was looking at some person he had not seen in a long time. "My name's Wilcott, Mark Wilcott, this here's mine," he said, motioning around the saloon, "and you look like hell. You seen the devil, have you?"

The stare continued as he said, "Or did you come over the mountain? I'm betting you saw a bit of Old Rocky clawing to be free of the mountain, falling down like it does every once in a while. Like to scare the hell outta me my first time coming this way. I won't go back up there. Once is enough of Old Rocky. It keeps trying to get back where it was all them centuries ago, before it got pushed up out of where it really belongs, right down here beside Oblivion."

Slade let it out. "I slid down the mountain on a sled of ledge, clear to the bottom. I never want to do that again."

"I can believe that, son. Mine weren't that bad, but like to scare me to death." He nodded a kind of welcoming salutation, like a club membership had been invoked for the young newcomer. "What brings you into the heart of Oblivion, son?"

"I'm looking for my father who was last heard of in the Great War, at West Point, Georgia. I haven't heard anything about him since '65 and the battle there in Georgia when the war was about over."

"What's his name, son?"

"Captain Jeremy Slade, same as me."

"Name is new to me, Jeremy. Never heard it here. What was it brought you all the way here from Georgia?"

"From Tennessee really. Just heard that he was taken by a family of Quakers when he was injured. He was declared as missing in action. We've never had a word about him, except some drummer years later said the Quaker family took in a few wounded back there."

"I don't know any Quakers hereabouts, Jeremy. Sorry about that." He poured another beer. "Here, this one's on me for your long trip. I got to admire you for the search. I can get you work here if you want, and you sure look like you can use it."

The two chatted while Wilcott served other customers and they were about to part when Wilcott, with a sudden inspiration it seemed, said, "What was the name supposed to be of them Quakers that came this way, Jeremy?"

"Murchin is all I ever heard. Murchin, from near West Point in Georgia."

Wilcott almost leaped over the bar top, exclaiming, "Dammit, boy, there's Murchins here, out the valley about ten, twelve miles, a covey of them, hard-working folk but I ain't never heard them being Quakers."

He gave Slade directions to their ranch, then added, "They had some injured kin when they came here, but I'd guess most of them died off. Check them out. I got some horses at the livery and you can use or buy one at a decent price if that's what you want. Tell Sven at the livery you can use one of my mounts. Northwest about 10 miles and they work like the world is gonna end before they can get enough for the whole family. I like them even though they don't spend too much time in here."

Outside, the sprawl of the town came at Slade. The two well-dressed ladies, coming back along the other side of the road, again eyed him. The barefoot boy with the hoop whooped it up down the center, dusty road of Oblivion. The whittling man, still intent on his piece of wood, worked his knife with ease, the sun still taking part as if at his hands.

Oblivion, for all of that piecemeal exposure, came off as better than he imagined but minutes before, for there came again to young Slade an awed and overpowering sense of knowledge, of acceptance. It was as powerful as what happened on the mountain, and it took his breath away, and was replaced immediately by a whole series of images that had accompanied him since his younger years; the shadow from his father's horse, the blue uniform against the paler sky, the eerie sense of loss of a man he did not really know, who lurked somewhere in his mind as only an existence ... so close but untouchable. His breath went again, in a deep exhalation.

At the livery an old man, with a huge mustache and a discernable limp, selected a mount for him. "Name's Blue Boy, a real decent animal. Wilcott, a Yankee man, gives all his horses Yankee names one way or the other, like he's still celebrating the war. He was in the war and wore all blue, as you might know. But a fair man. I was a Reb and hurt a bit and he let me work here, ever since he come here in '65 or '66."

The old man looked at Slade and said, "So you're borrowing a horse to ride where? Where you headed, son?"

"Out to Murchin's place. Wilcott says its northwest 10 miles."

"Decent ride, son, and them folks'll welcome you. They're good hardworking people don't come into town much except one or two of them. You a relative?"

"No," Slade answered, "just looking for my father who's been missing since the war."

"There's been enough of that, son. I sometimes wish someone would come looking for me, but I suspect all of them are gone now. Was all old even before the war. That settled down on me when I got here, leaving the war behind. It was a nasty piece of work I don't miss none at all." Tiredness, in an odd manner, had becalmed the old warrior, like fishing does or a campfire or a friendly game of cards between saddle pards. Time for reflection is found in each one of them, age having its rewards if taken so.

Slade, mounted on Blue Boy, started out of town, but he had not gone ten hoof beats of Blue Boy and the powerful sense of association hit him again. Again his breath, expelling itself as knowledge and anxiety, hit once more. The long-held images repeated themselves, the power of their recall coming down on him, or up out of him, as if he had been hit with a sledge. Might not it have been easier if his ride down the mountain had not been successful? The thought came on him and just as quickly left him. The sense of belonging came with an added hit; he wondered if he was being told this place should become home to him, after his long journey was over, if his search was fruitless, would this place called Oblivion become his home? There was no denying it had the power to exert a reaction in him.

Blue Boy, stepping off proudly, headed out of Oblivion, his step that of a military-trained animal. A bit of comfort approached young Slade the way pay-back is found in some situations.

The ride was a pleasant one and Blue Boy was a fine animal who had good instincts, knew the reins, and knew the gentle touch of hands and spurs of his rider, an agreement reached.

At least a mile before the Murchin ranch house came into site, Slade noticed how industrious and trim handwork and labor had been used in a number of places. The fence line was as straight as if a ruler had been used to set it, poles were straight as dies, and rails were as smooth as if found in a special forest. A sense of neatness made itself known, and the picture of the ranch house, as he gained a rise and saw it, spread like a picture across the end of a small valley. The scale of a small mountain sat behind it like a backdrop on a pictured scene. All of it warmed Slade as he approached the house and an older man sitting out front on a porch rocker. Nobody else was in sight, though a curl of smoke rose from one of the two chimneys on the house. The aroma of baking bread caught his attention, saying the kitchen was being used.

The old man waved, motioned Slade up to the porch. "Nice to have a visitor, son. I don't get to see many people. Pleasure to meet you." He thrust out his hand. "Name's Abel Murchin. This is home. You on a journey?" His face was round and pleasant and wore his years with a kind of grace that some men can carry with utmost dignity, as if the Lord's hand had found them.

"I've been looking for my father for a long time. His name is Jeremy Slade, as is my name. He was said to be missing in battle almost at the end of the Great War. He was a captain in the Union army and we have never had any final word on him."

"I'm sorry to hear that about your father, son. We took in a few soldiers who were wounded, but most of them have died on us. Whereabouts was your father missing?"

"At West Point, Georgia, near the end of the war, about the last month, I think."

Abel Murchin rose from his rocking chair, a huge grin on his face. "Melba," he yelled, "Melba, come out here quick."

He had Slade by the hand. "Sit down, son. Sit down. We came here from West Point a good many years ago. Brought a few of those wounded men with us, both Blue and Gray, and most of them passed on to the lap of their God. My daughter Melba can help you."

Happiness ran across his face as if he had won a long race, just as an anxious but composed woman came out of the house. Her apron was white with flour, as were her hands and arms, much of her face, and a good portion of her blouse. She looked to be in her forties, had a pretty face and wide eyes, and carried herself with a certain charm that Slade saw at once.

"What is it, Father?" she said. "You yelled louder than I've heard in a long spell. You have a surprise for me? Or a problem?" She smiled at Jeremy Slade.

"His name's Jeremy Slade and he's been looking for his paw for a long time. He went missing at West Point, Georgia almost at the end of the war and nobody's seen him or heard from him since, except he knows we brought some hurt soldiers to home back there."

"Oh, I am sorry," Melba said, "but I don't remember any Jeremy Slade. We had a few poor boys die after we took them in, but no Slade. What did he look like?"

"Oh," Slade said, "I don't really remember him. I was real young. The last I saw of him was him sitting his horse the day he left us, and that horse threw a dark cloud down on top of me like the world was going to end soon. But I'd guess he was a good-sized man, broad in the shoulders, was a hunter and a reader and knew his way with animals."

"Oh, I suppose we had a couple of men that fit such a description, but just about all of them have passed on. Some of them never finished the journey coming out here, but died on the way, none of them wanting any part of the battle anymore."

Slade, too long on his journey to let go, said, "You said that just about all of them passed on. I would guess that means some haven't. That's what I'd like to check before I move on, keep looking."

"Well, Jeremy Slade, you come to sit at our supper table, have a meal with us, and we'll see if we can help any at all. Come along." She looked at her father and said, "Ring the bell, Pa. It's time."

From nowhere is seemed, after Abel Murchin rang a bell four times, six young men and two girls in their teens materialized in the kitchen. The table could have sat half a dozen more guests, it was so long. They were a happy, industrious lot, Slade figured, all bearing the same facial characteristics, all in good health, all showing signs of some kind of work they had been at.

Abel Murchin introduced Jeremy Slade to the family, Melba lead them in thankful prayers, and Jeremy Slade knew a time of thankfulness and total comfort in the company of family of strangers.

After the meal was over, dishes cleared and tasks assigned and completed, Melba and her father led Slade into a comfortable sitting room. They had a discussion that lasted a full half hour, and Jeremy Slade, saying his deepest thanks, left for the town of Oblivion. Blue Boy answered his hands and his spurs with fleetness every once in a while.

Yet anxiety sat in the reins, and horse and rider both felt it.

As Slade entered Oblivion, the sun still visible in between distant mountain peaks, the prairie beyond town as if flooded by a golden sheen, he felt again the acceptance, the knowledge, the sense of belonging someplace, the same feelings he had before.

It was Melba's simple mention of the knife that did it, how it was the one thing that one of the wounded men held onto all these years, though he did not have all his memory.

That man with that knife looked up from his whittling as the young searcher stood before him. The knife with the red and gold handle worked away in his hands even as his eyes poured over a face that he had seen before, hundreds of times. He shook his head, trying to find his way to something hidden the way so many things over the years had been hidden.

Then it hit the whittler broadly, like a revelation. It was the face he had seen so many times in the mirror: the same eyes, the same set of cheekbones like golden twins, the same blond tresses and the same darker eyebrows. Finally, to cap off a full recall, the same tilt at one corner of the mouth where a smile lurked playfully.

Both men managed a momentary grin, and accepted warmth emanating from some dark space just behind the same sets of eyes, dim at first but promising.

And the war came and went again and a little boy down beside a giant horse walked through the opening shadow and hugged his father.

Josiah Weaverlake and the Dog Pack

"That damned dog almost bit my leg off." The cowpoke, Sledge Burke, noisy as his pals, and getting as drunk, swinging his arms around, was making excuses about a near fight with an old man beside the livery stable. He and his trail-hard pals, dust squeezing out where they walked and talked, were making a racket as they drank at Gee Buff's Open Tavern. The three young herders were hardly 20 years apiece, made room for themselves with false noise and bluster, and were therefore extended some tolerance by older hands in the saloon, men who had grown the same way with the same sudden leaps of confidence, and the same paltry mistakes.

"I accidentally bumped into the old patch and he smelled like a herd of dead sheep, like a sheep bath. All I was doin' was makin' sure my mount got his due at the livery. I thought this old codger was goin' to stink me up too, so I pushed him away and the dog, big as a small cow, came out of the dark like a shot. Got me right by the ankle, near tore my boot off. If I had my spurs in place I'd a kicked hell out of him, hound was big as a house."

Taking a big swig of beer, the white suds of the header marking his lips like a clown, Burke said to the bartender, "Hey, Keep, who's that old buck what's got that big dog? The one that smells like sheep dip I swear. He live around here? What's his brand?"

"Son, 'f I was you," Gee Buff the barkeep said, "I'd steer damned well clear that old man and his dog, which ain't no dog nohow you look at him. That one's mostly wolf... by his bite, by his bark, by his howl when the moon falls into the open window at night or slips down to touch your crotch or your toes when you're blanketed out there on the range. He's got pedigrees that don't need no countin' and no matterin' no way you look at it. Word is the old man, name is Josiah Weaverlake, found him scraggly as a bare bush up on Tuncon Pass a few years ago. Had busted a leg, he did. Had bad cuts or bites from some awed critter, and old Weaverlake fed him and nursed him, had him nights under his own blanket, and trained him to be a guard dog. He's apt to be that herder's best pal." Buff dropped his head to forecast a stern warning to the young dude still swinging his arms like a cow's tail at flies. He looked over his spectacles like a wise old man making points. "Be smarter than you 'pear to be right now, son; stay away from old Weaverlake. He's got more'n one a them dogs, I hear."

"Oh, somethin' will level the ground for them, that's for sure," the young cowboy Burke said, nodding at his pals, making the face of a know-it-all, the kind that wants to make you puke. "He better watch his manner the next time we pass by. I sure don't like that sheep dip smell gettin' on my duds." When he brushed down on his vest and shirt, the dust fell away from him in a small puff of gray matter.

Buff, of course, knew where he was coming from. He had seen the likes of him on so many nights he had lost count. He continued his warning. "Take it from me, son, that ain't the only dog, or wolf for that matter, Weaverlake's got. Has a passel of hounds, all breed-mixed, up there where he keeps his animals. That big one latched on to your ankle's got a few blood brothers mind Weaverlake's critters while he's about here on his needs."

Buff could feel the thick signs of his words being ignored by the cowpoke still sloppy at the bar.

Across the dry road through the center of town, a few buildings down, Josiah Weaverlake was loading his small two-wheel wagon with supplies from the general store. He was wearing a dark, thick, short coat he had not taken off all day. Leather boots stood up to just below his knees. A scabbard sewn into one boot carried a small, sharp knife. His mule Skinny was waiting to get back to a patch of grass in the canyon where the herder's sheep were kept penned by wire.

The storekeeper shook hands with the old man. "See you next time, Josiah. Use some of that soap you might get to see a woman some time." He laughed and patted the old man on the back.

"Lost all that interest a ways back, Myron. The bow don't string the fiddle much anymore."

They both laughed deeply, with mutual acceptance of each other, and the night slipped its cover down on them. The mule Skinny started out the back way from town and Josiah Weaverlake was asleep before the wagon was barely out of town, heading up the incline to home. A rifle rested under his feet on the wagon bed. The large dog, unseen, by any eyes, moved ahead of them. His name was Caesar.

Burke and his pals started early the next day to get rid of the trail's taste still hanging about them. Buff noted once in a while how they pushed their heads together and whispered. He suspected little good to come of such maneuvering, so he himself whispered to the sheriff about his suspicions.

The sheriff laughed lightly. "I ain't ever worried about old Weaverlake being alone up there, Gee, 'cause he ain't alone. You and me know that. The young uns'll get to know it too, one way or another, they want to find out."

So it was, with young foolish bravado, and liquor of odd sorts fueling it, that the three cowpokes slipped out of town and headed up the road where Skinny the mule had sauntered home with his sleeping rider the night before. In an hour's ride they were at the mouth of the canyon. They wanted to cut the wire and scatter the sheep into the hills. They wanted to laugh all the way back to the saloon. They wanted to get some more liquor before the night was over. One of them dismounted and approached the wire stands with a pair of wire cutters he had taken from his saddle bag. Their smell was in the air. The odor of oil was in the air from the wire cutters. The smell of their horses was in the air. Silence sat as still as a wet bush no longer thirsty.

The night was full of opposites.

Their horses felt it first, some intangible edge in the air, the night seeming to be alive with announcements of one sort or another. Burke at first ignored the snickers of his mount, the skittish feet prancing aimlessly, the reins coming taut in his hands, then he said, "Whoa, boy. Whoa. Easy now." The horse moved sideways, shook his rider as if their heartbeats were no longer together.

None of the young cowpokes wanted what came at them.

There was no noise. No howl or cry. No warning growls deep as night itself.

The riderless horse saw nothing, but knew the sudden flight right between its legs, a dark unseen rush of an unknown species full of terror and threat. The horse bolted and was downhill in a rush. The cowpoke with the wire cutters dropped them with a clink on a rock and started after his horse. Burke, almost thrown from the saddle, raced after his pal's mount. His other pal slipped a hand out and lifted his horseless pard onto his saddle and the pair of them also fled back toward town.

There followed after them, not wild critters but the noise of wild critters, barks and howls and cries from deep in the canyon and from the close-by hills where canine guards watched over the old man's holdings. The critter sounds chased the errant cowboys all the way to town.

The next night Gee Buff's Open Saloon, filled with customers, was noisy and raucous as usual. Burke and his two pals were standing at the far end of the bar, strangely quiet in the midst of the noise. Gee Buff and the sheriff were talking low at the other end, seeing now and then the looks coming back their way from the three young pards.

"Wonder what slowed them down to just breathin'?" the sheriff said. "Think we'll ever know? Them one's'll never tell us. It'll have to come from elsewhere."

Gee Buff looked up as the door opened. Josiah Weaverlake, still in his heavy coat and tall boots with the knife sheath, walked into the saloon and right up to the bar. Silence, like the night before, sat on top of everybody in the room.

Josiah Weaverlake, in his thick voice as though it was full of the ages, said to the barkeep, "Pour me a beer, Gee, if you will." Slowly, without any disdain in the movement, he placed the wire cutters down on the bar. "And give these back to whomsoever. I am not hiring anybody. I don't need no more sheep men. Tell 'em I got me enough sheep help."

Every man in the room knew the message had been delivered, with authority.

Last Stage from Crow's Hill

It all started when Gentleman John, a Comanchero of double mix, hot as his Mexican blood, cold as his Comanche stance, advised the mayor of Crow's Hill that he would attack the town at noon the next day. "I will burn the town to the ground and take all the horses," was written on a note in a decent and easily-read handwriting.

Texas maps, every one of them I've looked at, say Crow's Hill's not there anymore. Maybe it was never there, out there in the foothills of West Texas, but my grandfather, gone now close to 70 years, swore he was there the day before the last stage left Crow's Hill, bound for freedom and safety. The next morning, from a high point on Davis Mountain, he saw the stage just slide over the crowned road out of town when the attack came. Three extra horses traveled behind the stage in a tandem he'd never seen, but Crow's Hill, he said, went up in smoke that day. Some men had slipped out of town during the night and were never heard from again. Grandfather, a stubborn little Irishman, in broad daylight rode right at what was known as Gentleman John's stronghold in the hills. "They knew I was not running away from them, so they must have let me pass. I saw not one of them that day, and suppose they were massed elsewhere for the attack, or honored my brazen pride."

He also remembered some of the arguments about who was eligible for the stage. And it was a nice charity that picked passengers.

Some ladies were picked first, the few of them, along with the lone doctor in town. When he refused to accept the ride, the mayor said, "Doc, there might be nothing left here for you to fix when this thing is over, and two of those ladies are pregnant. Go where you'll be of some use."

The sheriff's widow, him dead less than a week from the Comancheros and her carrying their first child, was the first name to go on the list. She too refused the ride, but the mayor saw that as a little problem a bit of rope would take care, if it really would be necessary. Mrs. Hammond, the banker's wife, with a letter to be delivered, if ever, to a banker in Missouri with instructions for the dispersing of all Crow's Hill Bank's assets, which had been sent on secretly at least a month before ... on the same stagecoach. Mrs. Hammond, also carrying a child, and Jim Truex the driver, were the only people who knew about the earlier shipment.

The next on the list was Dawn Tilman, an actress of great talent who had been stranded in town by a crooked manager caught up in a crooked game. Jim Wilzer's son Joey, only 11 years old, also had a seat. The last guaranteed seat was drawn from a lottery, the profits from which were given to Truex for his pay. It amounted to $122, a princely sum for him if he got to destination. That seat went to Pit Wilfrey of the livery but he gave the seat to a man whose family was coming his way in a month, all the way from St. Louis. Pit, it was said, said he had to stay to make bullets, that he was too old for much of anything else except fighting back at something that bothered the hell out of him.

Gentleman John was doing just that.

Four months later, in Missouri, meeting Truex in a saloon, my grandfather heard about the last night and the eventual ride out of town.

"You saw us go, Johnny?" Truex said. "Where were you?"

"I rode out the day before, Jim, at high noon. I didn't steal away like some did. I headed out right for Gentleman John's hangout, out there in the foothills. Not one Comanchero came near me. Not a single one, which was a great surprise, and I saw you and the stagecoach clear the hill, there down beside Davis Mountain, and go out of sight. How was your ride? You have an adventure?"

Truex, Grandfather said, looked no worse than before, a gruff, sour-looking man who was known for his dedication and fierceness in the face of trouble. His hat was the same beaten sombrero, with the same bullet hole in the creased top he had worn the other times Grandfather had seen him. The same gun belt was at his waist this time, with the same pistols, the ones with pearl handles that a dying drummer gave him for his actions in a hold-up, keeping him alive as long as he could, standing over him like he was his guardian angel with six guns. Truex was known for a slow whip at the horses hauling out in front of his stagecoach, but fast with those pearl-handed guns.

"It was a quick and dusty ride for a few days until we met the soldiers coming our way, rushing to Crow's Hill, having cleared much of the trail behind them, and so for us. And then we relaxed at one waterhole station when Doc Nevers helped Mrs. Hammond deliver her first-born, a boy she immediately named Lester for his father she feared might already be dead back at Crow's Hill"

"What about the sheriff's wife? Her time come on the road?"

"She made it all the way to Sandhill and met up with an uncle. I last saw her going off in another wagon. Never saw her again."

"All the others?"

"The doc went on to St Louis or New Orleans, I'm not sure which. Joey Wilzer, the boy, is with some relatives. The lady actress is with another troupe. My shotgun headed back to Illinois after having his fill this time. And the gent who was looking for his family coming to Crow's Hill met them on the road like it was a miracle, I swear. What a celebration that was, like a real shivaree happening right on the damned road. Damndest thing I ever saw. It don't happen that way much. Not likely. He joined them and they turned right around and headed back home. His wife was greatly relieved, I do believe. I can say we all fared better than Crow's Hill did, everybody on that coach coming out of there that last day."

He paused and added, "Like you, Johnny, heading off to meet Gentleman John like you did." He stopped talking, took another sip, and continued with his scheme of life. "Never know when a damned decent drink might be your last, so enjoy the taste and the full expectation, like you did, moving right at Gentleman John's roost."

"Not exactly with those expectations," Grandfather said. "I did have some hopes riding with me. What have you heard from Crow's Hill? I was with a skinner much of this time since we left there. Kept me busy, he did. Fed me. Paid me with due. But we never heard a word because we saw nobody except Indians the whole time. He knew them all, so it was a relaxable time even though the work was dirty. I was plain hungry when I came across him and his fire, like it was heaven's gate waiting for me. You hear any news from back there?"

"Leveled," said Truex, "Crow's Hill gone right to the ground, every building, the jail, the livery, like they was never there. I've talked to at least two people that Gentleman John let go, there was a bunch of them, but not a one with a horse or a gun. 'Walk home,' he said, pointing east, 'and leave us alone. This is Comanche country.' Said he got more than 400 horses in the raid, a couple of hundred rifles and hand guns, and burned down a few ranch houses in the mix. Don't know how many cows went along for the walk, whole ranches moving. I don't think the banker even had a good count on what was where."

He shook his head and added, "Gonna need a lot more troopers out that way 'fore I make the move. Oh, I'm going back in due time, figuring it's my calling of sorts, but I won't rush things until I hear Gentleman John's caught his due. That dude, though named proper, is owed one way or another by a lot of people, but I don't want for a minute to get on his bad side, all the getting even he contemplates, even with all the lucky stars he throws around like he was God hisself."

"No other news from out that way?"

"Just heard that Comanche bigs like Quanah Parker escaped a large search party, him and his pal Kwahada. Them's the ones wouldn't sign the Medicine Lodge Treaty back in '67. Gentleman John's in cahoots with those dudes, like a sidekick of sorts. Guns and horses the main barter and whole herds of cows, wiping out ranches like they was Crow's Hill to boot."

That's when grandfather said that Truex changed the trend of the conversation in one breath, and asked, "Have you heard anything about me and my passengers other than what I've told you?"

Grandfather said no and Truex said, "I took my money and spent it all, or gave some of it to those moving on with not a cent in their pockets, but I have to tell you I had some extra passengers that was not part of the original deal made in Crow's Hill. I stopped the other side of the hill where you saw me down along Davis Mountain and hauled six more bodies on board after the others agreed we could dump some of their baggage. In fact, most of it we tossed, along with some sad looks, I'll tell you, way some ladies can be. I told them they had to dump the sour looks because we had more at stake than styley dresses or boots."

He took another drink, as if to gather himself in recall, but was still the gruff and loyal driver he had always been. That was his badge, a badge of honor he could wear with pride, as Grandfather believed until his time had passed; that Truex was a perfect example of what honorable gents good cowboys are, those who work hard for their bosses and give their all, even their lives if called on.

Truex added, "Three older boys with rifles we put flat on top and had one in the rear boot. One more lady and a cripple we put in the carriage on the floor. It was hell for a ride, but we all got through, even carrying the newborn who had to be fed along the way, the way you might picture it."

When Truex was asked by Grandfather if they had to shoot at anybody on the way, he said, "Three hombres in phony serapes, like they was trying to look the part of Comancheros or Mexicans, jumped from behind a tight turn in the trail. They was masked with red bandanas on their faces, but the actress said she recognized one of them as a gent she had talked to after one performance, recognizing the belt buckle he wore. She called him by name and when the three boys on top rose up with their rifles they scattered like they was shot. That's the only excitement we really had outside a coyotes finishing off a dead horse. Saw no sign of its rider, though the saddle was still on the animal. The banker's wife led a prayer for that unknown rider, wherever he was. That was special to me. Made me think I was doing good."

Grandfather asked if there was anything else.

Truex said, as if it sounded like the last thing he ever said to my grandfather, "Nothin' except my shotgun's headed back after a week on the road heading home. Said the west was too big and too exciting for him to go back and sit on a porch in Illinois. Sent me a wire and I'll see him in a day or two."

Grandfather always said the west was opened by special men who knew what they were up to and why. I can still see him listening to the Lone Ranger and Tonto on the radio, the little red dial light like a spark in his room, and him in his rocking chair making hardly a peep at all, listening, having all these memories until his very last day.

Linked

Shaking his head, confounded, disbelieving what he was seeing, Sheriff Wade Gordon stood over the dead man, his face beaten and torn as if some beast of malevolent proportions had committed the murder.

Turning to his young deputy, Clay Simmons, a still-green youngster wearing a bright badge, highly impressionable, but a good man with a gun and on a horse, the sheriff said, "This ain't a bit natural, Clay, what I'm looking at. It sure ain't natural."

"I never seen a man who died like this, Sheriff. Looks like he was clubbed to death. Had holy hell beat out of him. Ain't much left of his nose, both ears ripped like rags, and I don't know where his teeth have gone, at least most of them. I don't see a one of them on the ground."

"There are a few other things you ain't picked up yet, Clay. You got to take in everything you see. I don't care if it looks like nothing, if it's something, remember it." He laid a look on his deputy as if he was saying, "Make darn sure you understand everything I say to you. Some day you'll get to carry the load."

"I just don't know what you're getting at, Sheriff. He's dead. He got the hell beat out of him. Must have had a helluva fight with someone way out here from town. He ain't going to tell us anything, nothing more than having his horse sit over there off the trail like there was nothing wrong to begin with."

Gordon stood back from the body on the ground, which was a regular cowpoke they could not identify as yet because his face was beaten so viciously the job would be difficult for the dead man's best friend, or even his brother.

"Remember what I'm saying, Clay. This poor cowpoke was not in a fight on the ground. He was knocked right out of his saddle, like a board hit him in the face at high gallop or he run into a low tree limb on the dead run. Wham! Down and out and dead, maybe even before he hit the ground. His clothes can tell you that, like he just came from town, had a bath at Maizie's place, got his clothes washed or changed, whatever, and headed back to whatever ranch he worked on or some trail drive now heading home."

"Okay, Sheriff, I guess I saw none of that. I got a lot of learning to get done yet."

"Let's get him into Henry Seaver's in town, get him ready for burial after we see if someone can tell us who he is, if he got some bad enemy hanging on him for a long time. I don't think this is any accident."

"Like someone was waiting out here on the road for him?"

"Something like that, Clay. Maybe exactly like that."

In the junction town of Barnstead, in the shadows of the Rockies near sundown, it did not take long to find the identity of the dead man on display at the coffin maker's place, under a sign rigged by Seaver at the direction of the sheriff; "Tell us who this man is. We don't know him. He was murdered. Sheriff Gordon."

Curiosity, of course, makes the rounds in a hurry in most all towns on the trail. Barnstead was no different than the others, with the word running from saloon to livery to general store to hotel lobby to the restaurants on a couple of sites. It was not a hushed reverence, but morbid curiosity at first. "Someone's dead at Seaver's place. Nobody yet knows who he is."

It was just before dark when a cowpoke came to the sheriff's office. "That dead fella over at Seaver's place is Lucas Bench, Sheriff. I rode twice or three times with him. Once at the Lazy R and then for Mangan's last drive all the way up the trail to Catlo. I swear to God it's him. And he's got the same bent little finger Lucas got as a kid, from what he said one night at a campfire. It's twisted right at the big joint. He got it in a jackknife fight. I haven't seen him in a few months."

Three days later, the town generally quiet as summer crawled into fall, slow motions coming on the earth, another body was found on the road from Brimler. The body had the same type of menacing injuries, and the cause of death was also apparent, a face beaten beyond recognition. It took nearly a week to find out the dead man's identity, a deputy from up in the northern part of the territory, a lawman who had never been this far south in any of his duties.

The deputy's identity was confirmed by telegraph, from a description of the man's scars, because all personal identification had been removed from his body, but a sum of money, currency and coin, was still in his pockets, about $20. That would be enough to carry him for a week in town, with a bath and shave, food and drink, and a roof over his head. The purpose of his trip was not disclosed in the telegraph, except that "he was on business of this office."

Sheriff Gordon, approached by the mayor and bank owner, Burt Ringwald, about the two dead men, told the mayor that he was working on the cases. "Doing my best, Mayor. Not much to go on. Looks like he was in a fight out there on the trail and got knocked pretty silly. Maybe clubbed by a board or a log or some other contraption I ain't thought of yet." The sheriff did not let on about any of his temporary conclusions he had shared with his deputy. Those points, he argued, he'd keep to his office, meaning him and his deputy.

Ringwald was a different kind of a dude as far as some people were concerned, stand-offish at times, too much of a braggart at other times, and a man who fiddled too much on some matters around town.

What he did was run a pretty solid bank for a few years. The bank came first, the town second, if things were looked at with a measuring eye.

"This kind of activity has got to stop, Sheriff." The mayor's voice rang out in front of a lot of townsfolk. "I want you to make sure you do all in your power to find the reasons behind these murders. I'll try to get the council to let you appoint another deputy if you need one, maybe two or three of them."

He shook his head to show his disgust and added, "Pretty damned gruesome for my taste." He paused again and Gordon could practically read him as he continued, by saying, "You get yourself and the deputy out there patrolling the road. Like I said, I'll argue with the council to get you more help if you ask for it. But do something." He walked off shrugging his shoulders as if he was the most disgusted man in the town.

Ringwald was a tall, well-dressed man on every occasion, as if he would not dare be caught with his guard down, like wearing denim pants or a sweaty shirt or work gloves. Word around the town was that his clothes, every single piece, came special delivery all the way from St. Louis or Chicago or further away, the way rumors get rolling on a gent who generally has things going his way.

The sheriff, like a few other people in Barnstead, had little respect for the mayor because of his real indifference to most matters concerning common townsfolk. Like the time there was a gunfight at a rich rancher's corral and the mayor tried his best to keep it quiet or treat it as a mere circumstance. The rancher was a big investor in the bank who deserved special attention in all matters, in whatever way the mayor or the bank president could arrange it.

The murdered deputy from up north, "in Barnstead on business," was finally buried on instructions from his sheriff. "He was a good man. Treat him well and put him in a decent box. I'll pay. Sent by Term Alexander, Sheriff of Winfield."

When the third and fourth bodies turned up, one on a section of less-traveled trail, and another on the wide grass east of town, Ringwald came at Sheriff Gordon every chance he could, including railing away at him on the open boardwalk on two consecutive afternoons. The cause of death in each incident was the same as the previous trail murders, a smashing, mashing beating no man deserved.

One of the dead men was identified right away from his odd dress, a drummer about his business; the other remained unknown and might have been a stranger or saddle tramp, or a cowpoke looking for work. He was buried as "Unknown Rider" sketched on his marker. His horse, also found wandering, was given to Henry Seaver in lieu of expenses expended for the pine box and the burial.

Two events came about that Sheriff Gordon had not expected, but the kind of help no man can refuse, though he has no idea of its coming.

The first was the appearance of a saddle bum, but without a saddle, as he proclaimed later on, though he did lug a wrapped contraption on his back in a kind of framework carrier. Small, wiry, looking thinner than he might want to be, dressed as poorly as one can imagine for the times, the young man walked into Gordon's office one evening, looking confused, hungry, thirsty, a man out on his own, down on his luck.

"Sheriff, I can't swear by everything I'm gonna tell you, but I believe I saw it happen." He looked back over his shoulder and pointed that way. "East of town."

Gordon, searching for facts first in his order of things, said, "What's your name, son, and where did you come from? How did you get here? Where's your horse? I don't see one outside."

The streak of explanations started. "My name is Bordon Maximus. I started out in Chancellorsville about four years ago and I've been moving and stopping and moving since then."

"What's that gear you carry on your back?"

The young man said, "That's my sleeping quarters, Sheriff. It's a rope hammock of sorts. I usually sleep in it when it's hung from a tree or from big rocks close enough to do so. I got two iron hooks and extra rope and it does me fine. And I got a hunk of canvas I can hang over me. It's a lot cheaper than any hotel and as safe as it can be, seeing as I've got this far in my travels."

Gordon got the impression that Maximus would carry on if he was not slowed down.

He pushed a chair at his visitor. "Sit," he said. "What'd you see out there, son, east of town?"

"Well, Sheriff, I lost my horse a few nights earlier when a mountain lion got him, and had to hide my saddle, and so I was walking. It got near to dusk and I hung my rig in a clump of cottonwoods. I was well off the ground and I figured I was due a good night's sleep. I could feel it coming on me. Not long after I was up in the air, just about to go off to sleep, when I heard some noise. It was not far from me, and it was a horse. Then I saw a man go behind the trees a ways from me and change his duds. Took them off down to his birthday suit and got some other clothes out of his saddle bags."

"Is that all?" Gordon said. "That ain't much."

"Well, I didn't think it was either, but then he just sat back and stayed still, like he was listening for something. Then I heard it too ... hoof beats on the trail, someone coming, not galloping along, but moving steady, sort of. This gent had his hand over his horse's mouth so he won't make noise, and waits until a rider passes by on the road. Nothing else is moving out there. The rider goes by, this changed dude starts out to follow the other rider and pulls something from his saddlebag and starts to swing it over his head as he chases the other rider, like he scared the hell out of him. I thought it was a rope, the way he swung it over his head in a loop, and then he got close and just knocked that other rider right out of the saddle with that thing he was aswinging. Then he looked down on him lying out on the ground, looked through his pockets, didn't take a thing, and just rode off like he had just picked his share of beans or cotton for the day. Just rode off. Just like that."

He snapped his fingers.

Gordon made notes in a little covered pad he carried in his shirt pocket. Even the deputy had never seen it.

That was the first event.

The second came on the following night.

It was providential at first, then went quickly to good law work.

Sheriff Gordon, leaning on the rail, in the saloon, having the first of his two or three nightly drinks, saw the stranger enter the saloon. The new man carried himself with a certain air, a certain flair, that Gordon measured on the spot, saw him as a specially qualified man, as a cohort, a man on a mission. He was not a saddle tramp. He was not a cowpoke or drover on the end of a drive. He gave off an aura.

Conscious of something working in himself, Gordon turned to face the stranger, the badge on Gordon's chest fully exposed.

The stranger, cool, calm, not at all uneasy in a new place among strangers, gave a hardly perceptive nod to Gordon as if he was saluting his badge and the role in life that it represented. With a smooth but unnoticeable move, he changed his direction and came close to Gordon at the bar. Something was palmed in his hand. For a bare second he flashed it alone to Gordon. It was a sheriff's badge.

Gordon felt good about his own quick judgment.

He said, "Excuse me, Sheriff. Do you know what the 'term' cohort means, in the special sense? The real 'Term.'"

Barnstead Sheriff Wade Gordon knew he had been, on the sly, introduced to Term Alexander, Sheriff of Winfield, working on the death of his deputy, staying out of the public eye as much as possible, an undercover man, if you will, bent on solving the murder of what was obviously a good and loyal deputy.

He felt the kinship and the weight of the task.

In his room at the hotel late in the night, Gordon shared all his thoughts with Sheriff Alexander. He also showed him his little notebook in which he had entered every single thought that came to him about the murders. Bordon Maximus's recounting of his trail observation also brought a serious display of interest from the northern sheriff.

He went back to Gordon's notebook, looked off as if an apparition was visiting in the room and demanded attention.

"Who's showing the most interest in these matters, Wade?"

"I'd have to say the mayor, Burt Ringwald. He's also the owner and president of the bank. He dogs me a lot, comes down on me in public a number of times. I discount most of it as his political side forcing the issue, but the man bothers me on other points. I just don't like him, and his all-for-me routine."

Alexander smiled innocently, nodded some kind of internal acceptance, and said, "Let me tell you something else that I am aware of." He looked around for a bottle, his mouth open, saying, "I'm bone dry."

Sheriff Gordon produced a bottle and each man took a jigger of whiskey and set it beside them on a little table.

"I know of a case where some senseless murders, seemingly without connection, not linked at all, were performed in a distant town. The local sheriff was hassled into spending all his energy and that of his deputies, scouring the countryside. They never found anything, but one day, when they were out gallivanting, the bank was robbed, at high noon, at the point of good business. The president of the bank blew out of town and nobody's seen him since. The bank closed down. It hasn't re-opened yet. It may not."

He sipped the jigger of whiskey, set the glass down and said, "I bet you don't know what the man's name was, the bank president's name."

"Not a clue," Gordon replied.

The huge grin Alexander offered up was a giveaway. "I believe we have a connection. A link."

Alexander finished off his jigger of whiskey. "Baron Waldwick," Alexander said. "Does that make you think of anything?"

"Sure does. Baron Waldwick is not very different from Burt Ringwald, like the two names are really connected, that they are linked, that they carry one identity, but it would be hell to prove."

"Our two heads are better than his one," was Alexander's reply. "All we need to do is plan things right, have some patience, and we've got him in the squeeze."

Gordon said, "How do we start?"

"When he's busy, we ought to check out the barn at his place."

"What do we look for?"

"That thing that Maximus said he saw the strange horseman swinging over his head."

Gordon was still unsure of things. "What is it?"

"Our connection, our link to all the crimes, here and up north," Alexander replied, "a rugged length of chain."

Sheriff Gordon vaguely saw the plan developing, but could feel its success. "If we find it, how do we link the link to the crimes?"

Sheriff Alexander, shaking his head slowly, mindful of what he was about to say, said, "I hate to wait for another death, but I get the impression that Ringwald or Waldwick is about ready to make his major play. If there is another murder and he screams to bloody hell about getting out there, I'll bet that's when the bank is hit by his gang or his hired guns; when the law is out of town."

"And we head out, but we only pretend to do so. And I'll hire you as a deputy. We'll just go and double-back, catch them in the act. Is that how it should go?" Gordon had a smile on his face.

"Let's hope it does, Sheriff. I've waited for this guy for a long time. I lost a good man because of him."

Nothing could have made Sheriff Wade Gordon feel any better as he went off to sleep that night.

A few days later, it all fell into play as another badly whipped body was found outside of town, again on the Brimler road.

The mayor screamed his own bloody murder at Sheriff Gordon, right on the main street of the town. The whole town must have heard him.

The law started out of Barnstead in a rush, the sheriff and his two deputies.

The law was on hand when the robbers came out of the bank. And out of town, on the stage that left carrying Mayor and bank president Burt Ringwald in a flight as part of the theft of his own bank, was unknowingly accompanied by two men who had been deputized by Sheriff Gordon, "just in case," as he told the mayor.

Kid Bullet and the Gainful Ministry

The voice came from the dark side of the street across from the Busted Leg Saloon, from deep in the shadows. "Hey, Sheriff, hey you, Kid Bullet, you ready to face a real grown-up man with them guns of yours? Come out and find the man daring you. Show your luck, Sheriff, your beginner's luck." A few pedestrians moving along the boardwalk, not seeing the source of the voice, but hearing it clearly in the soft night, ducked into any alley or open doorway they could find.

Trouble was afoot in town.

It was late in the evening in Winslow Hills, in the Wyoming Territory, on the verge of grassland and foothills beginning their long stretches. A middling breeze raised unseen dust on the road in and out of town, and a faint suggestion of a crescent moon hung its lower curve on the high brim of Mount Tobar. But it was too rare to throw much moonlight onto the town buried in shadow and dimness, more than half the places of business dark, and many lamps and candles blown out. A busy day getting ready to fall into deep sleep.

At 21, Travis Henry had become the sheriff in Winslow Hills, a small but likeable town in the territory. The election was a runaway, the one opponent being 50-year old Gus Lamond, who would never be able to handle the job, but he gave the sagest advice to the new lawman: "Don't be bigger than who you are, so make the smallest target, the smallest shadow you can. Don't give away your shadow, but stay in the shadows if possible, use them; it'll make the job a lot easier to get done."

Lamond also had the keenest eye in Winslow Hills, always alert to change, circumstance, and accompanying characters that kept the town in motion, but held most of what he saw to himself. Trust was generally hard to impose on people; he had found that out a long time in the learning.

In truth, there was a history already bound up in local talk about the new lawman. That history had been building for more than a decade. He had come into the job, because of those stories, for Travis Henry was called, now and forever, Kid Bullet, with the inevitable stories attached.

Before he was 12 years old, Travis Henry had three errant bullets enter his slim body, each wound treated quickly so they were not fatal. Twice the wild bullets had found him on the trail as his family headed west, the wagon train attacked on two occasions, and Travis caught in the thick of it both times. One round ended up in his left thigh, from which he evinced no limp whatsoever, and the other lodged superficially in his upper left arm and was dug out by a woman on the train who had prior experience in retrieving slugs from the human body. It was said in ensuing years that the youngster never cried out during the extraction.

The third bullet, and the one that kicked off the Kid Bullet story becoming a legend in jail cells, trail drives and night campfires, railroad gangs, saloons full to the brim on Saturday evenings, happened outside a bank in the Wyoming Territory when robbers began firing randomly to back up their demands. The gang was the Lucky Fursten Gang, which turned out to be not so lucky on that occasion, as they ended up in jail, but had their name forever linked with Travis Henry. One of the Fursten bullets smashed the bank window and found young Travis across the street helping to load supplies onto the family wagon. Travis was in front of his father, when the shot came through the bank window, as if he'd been set in place with his arms angled just so that bullet found his hand and saved his father. That, as some old timers relate, is how stories begin about heroes and all that goes with them.

For it was that bank incident that assured early in his adolescence the name Kid Bullet came upon him, like a mantle thrown over his shoulders, and him being bound to wear it.

In school every boy wished the nickname was his own; they enacted thrills and deeds with it, from play-acting to staged duels where the name leaped from young throats. And the girls, bright and talkative and dreaming themselves onward, and brimmed with shiny eyes, looked upon him with heavy favor; he was a good-looking, fair-haired youngster, no bigger than his classmates, no smarter in the classroom apparently, but equipped with a special confidence that came earlier than usual to boys his age.

The girls knew it before all others, tuned into the message being emitted. One of them, Clarissa Mayes, with a concentration all her own, set her eyes, and heart, on Travis Henry for the long haul. Her father was one of the large ranch owners in the area and a most stubborn man.

Old Lamond thought for a long while that Travis Henry's nickname was a misnomer, but he saw Clarissa's intentions from a distance and kept them in the back of his mind; women, from whatever way they develop, often have the most scrutable eye.

As it was, the accumulation of those three wayward shots also left Travis Henry with a false sense of invincibility ... he would live forever, he believed, in the hands of the gods, however many there were, or what name was given them; and he carried no scars of those early wounds as evidence. Both statements carried with them the eventual tests on their validity, from glory-seekers, fast guns, and the inquisitive men used to the old saying, "Seeing is believing."

Albert Henry, Travis's' proud father, came up a problem every time he opened his mouth, boasting about his son and how he'd change things around Winslow Hills and in the territory in general. Not for once did he consider his son lucky to be alive in hard times, never mind becoming the sheriff.

"That boy of mine will outlast any sheriff we've ever had, that's for sure. It's a good thing we didn't elect that old man who sits his days out on his porch and in the sun. Some god up there favors my son. I don't know how far up he is, but he's reached down here and touched Travis like no boy's been touched I know of. Been that way for years. Let me tell you about that time when we were beset by villains and thieves wanting all our goods on the wagon train."

With a flair for the dramatic, with the storyteller's ability to build up momentum and concern in his tales, he'd append to the story a dire pronouncement, "Probably our women too." Such simple words extended the influence of each tale, and so those tales grew.

"Travis caught one that time and didn't even cry. That I'll swear to." He looked overhead, at some level of the divinities, tapped his forefinger repetitively down on the bar in the most declarative manner, before he swallowed his next shot of whiskey in quick gulp.

Off in a corner, smiling softly to himself, Gus Lamond, long on heavy thought and the human puzzle, quick in his mind and slow on his two feet and with his two guns, found appreciation in the elder Henry's presentation and storytelling.

Lamond realized the most important element in the whole story had never been mentioned by the man, or by any other townsfolk of Winslow Hills, that being the question of young Henry's ability with either hand gun or rifle. The subject, seemingly innocent at the present time, had never come up, and Lamond assumed that failing arose from "the invincibility of the new sheriff and the hands of the gods on him." Every citizen in the town had bandied the name about as if it was the word of the High and Mighty Himself.

The whole scenario had a ringing charm and hope in its company. But Lamond, half a century of life, experience and knowledge packed away in his saddle bag, figured some information lingered that he so far could only assume. He'd wait and see.

He'd keep his eye on young Henry, on the girl who obviously loved him, hoping, like many of the older set wanting to see the young breeds move on in life.

Travis Henry, it was apparent to Lamond, would have to outlive the badge, his father's tall tales, his nickname, a nearly hidden love affair, and threats that are often born and appear in shadows for lawmen all over the west.

And so it was, as we go back to the beginning in the saloon the night of his election, still sipping a beer too warm for enjoyment, knowing a sense of elation moving in him, that the new sheriff heard his name called from outside, and the first openly-declared use of his nickname.

"Hey, Sheriff, hey you, Kid Bullet, you ready to face a real grown-up man with them guns of yours?"

Even before Henry recognized the voice, he assumed correctly it could only be fast gun, big-mouth cowpoke at times, Turkey Trainor, mean, ugly as two buzzards with one piece of meat, but only when he was drunk. Trainor had been, for a good spell of his 30-ish years, the Saturday Drunk, a nickname he enjoyed immensely on that weekend day, but hated otherwise. He was lucid enough this night to compare it with Kid Bullet and the difference sent him into a bad spin.

It was 7 of the evening, early for many men to slide up to the bar, but Henry knew that Trainor had been in town all day, that gruff and thickening voice reaching him several times in the late afternoon, from the livery, the general store as he purchased a supply of bullets, and from the saloon before the supper hour.

As much as an echo, Henry heard Gus Lamond's words search him out of nowhere. "The shadows" of the message came as clear as a new lamp lit in a dark tunnel.

He yelled out to the road, "Hey, mister, I hear you. Wait'll I finish my drink and I'll be out pronto."

He slipped behind the bar, went out a rear door, crossed behind several buildings, heard a horse nicker in the livery, and then another pick up the call, crossed the dusty road in dusky shadows, and came up behind the building where Trainor had secreted himself.

It had taken him no more than three minutes, and he was mere feet from Trainor who impatiently gave away his place of recess, standing behind two boxes of burlap bags waiting for pick-up. He made no assessment of the man's selection of a stand or his intentions or the state of his character, other than he was drunk and most likely would live to regret any harm he caused.

Travis Henry, silent as a housebreaker, slipped in behind Trainor, slammed the handle of his own revolver on Trainor's wrist, heard the man grunt with pain and his gun fall to the boardwalk, whipped his own gun up at Trainor's chin, heard the thud, and shoved the collapsing drunk over the two boxes. Both guns were holstered, Trainor draped over his shoulder. With the potential bushwhacker thus arrested, Henry walked out of the deep shadows and went directly to the jail.

In the morning, under a bright sun, Henry gave his prisoner the first cup of hot coffee when he woke up.

With two gestures, one heavy and one light, he had gained a friend, and a slew of admiration from some of Winslow Hills' citizens.

One such citizen was Clarissa Mayes, her love growing deeper by the day, who told the story over and over again in the presence of her parents, her kid brothers, and any ranch hand who listened. She was coming on 18 years of age, wanted marriage before anything else, and let her parents know it. And there was a continuing sense of beauty and desirability emerging about her person that made it a good possibility of marriage, maybe sooner than later.

Her father announced on several occasions, "Not without a churchman, whenever the time comes, and hopefully that will be well down the line from now. There'll be a churchman or no wedding in this family." He spoke with vaunted assurance, as there was no church in Winslow Hills, one not seen in the near future, and a rare visit by any man of the cloth.

She never told her father or mother that she had been seeing Travis Henry on occasion, though her mother sensed a change in her daughter. She too withheld her intuitive feeling.

When one of Clarissa Mayes' younger friends was caught stealing from the general store, Henry covered for her, pulling the "taken" money from his own pocket. To cover the loss, he told her. Only Gus Lamond was aware of the exchange, and then Clarissa when her friend told her the story. Now, without doubt, Travis Henry had to become her husband. He was precious, kind, understanding, and entirely suitable for her; life would be a charm with him.

No more than a week later the Trainor incident, a shot rang out in the dawn flash. Henry, fitfully trying to sleep on a cot in the jail, and not having much luck, coffee not even on yet, leaped from a deep sleep, heard yelling, grabbed his hat and gun belt and ran toward the livery, where he thought the shot had come from.

Efram Hornbelt, the livery man, was yelling in the road. "I don't know where he went. I don't know who he is. I don't think I ever saw him before, but he tried to steal one of my horses and I shot at him. I don't know where he ducked out. He could have run out the back of the livery. He could still be in there. I don't know, but he didn't get my horse, that's for damned sure. He wanted the big black."

With caution, and trying to get what sleep evidence there was out of his eyes, Henry went into the livery, gun drawn, separating where he could shadow from substance, shade from reality. He heard nothing, not even the mice at work or play, or the owl high in the peak of the structure where he could see all below him.

It was a single strand of straw, floating from above like a forlorn leaf, that grabbed Henry's attention, and held it in place; he realized someone might be directly overhead in the loft, gun in hand, fear working his veins. He wondered what the supposed horse stealer was thinking. It came fast on what he had thought but a minute earlier.

He was less than two weeks onto his new job, the badge a shiny button on his vest, and his guns still holstered; he had yet to fire a shot as sheriff of Winslow Hills. Some thought it a strange thing, a sign of a coming time, an omen to be found in the sheriff's make-up, in his abilities.

In the middle of the livery, in the faint shadows in some spots, a lamp lit outside the door, he thought of Clarissa, the way he always did ... in a hurry, in some measurement, in a way he thought of no one else in Winslow Hills. He'd do nothing foolish, he said to himself, looking forward to seeing her again, thinking of the life with her in the coming happy years. He knew he could get caught up in such thoughts, for here he was with a thief or a horse stealer who might be on hand, who might be right above him.

As quick as Clarissa had come upon him, she departed with the strand of straw floating like a needle of light down beside him. With a shot up into the floor of the loft, he might shake the man loose ... and night draw the man into a shoot-out. But nothing was stolen, not as yet. He thought seriously on that point.

Loudly, he yelled to the livery man, saying very clearly, "Efram, I think he got away out the back, so close that door after you and fix it so he can't get back in here if he's the tricky sort. I'm going out the back door and see if I can get an idea where he went. He can't have gone far. Now lock that door good, Efram. I'll be out back."

Henry made enough noise to influence the man overhead he was leaving by the back door of the livery, slammed it tight, and stood still in the spot. He breathed slowly, lightly, not moving a muscle. He heard the mice moving. Outside an owl made comment. A carriage went down the main road in town and he could picture it stopping at the general store rather than at the saloon. For a good 10 minutes he stayed that way, his muscles itching to move, trying to exert themselves, rebelling against his silent, motionless stance. His eyes almost became accustomed to the deepest shadows where he could identify bridle and harness and assorted equipage, and two saddles sitting over a stall wall.

Lamond, having heard the shot as well, went out on his front porch, but no further; his legs making the determination, his guns hanging inside where they'd apparently be for the rest of his life. But he was again the eagle looker, and stayed in place on the porch.

He had kept all things to himself, while watching the young sheriff at his work. The times, he knew, were changing; they were not like the wild gun-shooting days of trail drive finishes, of personal confrontations that drove men to shoot-outs, those stupid quick draw circuses that saw death as the only result and no other decision coming forth. Even though there was greed and avarice about land and grass and fences and no fences, and the introduction of sheep to the wide grass, the advances of one element served only to change the times in a permanent manner.

He wondered what the sheriff was up to.

When a soft movement gave off a sound overhead, Henry froze still again against the back wall, right near the door. He waited.

The man overhead moved slowly, came to the ladder leading down from the loft, managed to carelessly kick loose a few more strands of straw, and started down the ladder, his searching boots making the most sound so far. He was stealth itself when he came to the bottom of the ladder, and began taking soft steps across the floor toward the back door. With one hand out in front of him to push the door open, his hand gun in his hand right near the sheriff, he pushed the empty hand slowly forward, and Henry slammed his gun hand with his revolver.

The grunt of pain was loud, as was the immediate whack on his head from Henry, dropping him to his knees, his gun already gone from his hand.

In 10 minutes the man was behind bars, screaming about a cowardly sheriff afraid to face him.

Henry, relaxed, looking up as Gus Lamond entered the jail, said to the prisoner, "Just like the coward you are, trying to steal a horse from an old man. Wait'll they hear that about you in court, because you'll be facing the judge soon enough. You're lucky you're not facing a real theft or that you shot somebody. There'd be a long time before anybody would see you."

He nodded at Gus Lamond who walked right to the cell and said to the prisoner, "You're mighty lucky, is right, son. Mighty lucky."

He figured it was time to spring the news to the whole town through one man. "Let me tell you how lucky you are, son. Sheriff Henry here is the fastest gun I have ever seen in all my years. I have watched him long before he became sheriff. He was making hay all the time with his gun. So fast at times he made me dizzy watching him from long range."

Then the wisest man in all of Winslow Hills took Sheriff Henry into one corner of the office and, in a low voice, said, "Is it true that Clarissa's father won't let her get married without a man of the cloth."

Surprised at first, then realizing the man in front of him knew more than any other man in the town, he said, "That's right, Gus. He's said that to Clarissa until he's red in the face and she's gone into tears. I don't know what we'll do. And she wants marriage more than I wanted this badge."

"Well," said Gus Lamond, I hope things work out for both of you before something ungainly happens." He smiled, nodded as if he had made a deal with himself, shook hands with the sheriff, said to the prisoner, "Luck may not be enough for you, son. And guns ain't ever going to do it for you, not in this town."

He left the sheriff's office and headed for the livery.

It was a quiet week later, the prisoner sentenced to two months in jail by the judge, that a handsome black stallion road up to the Mayes ranch house, and the rider said to Mrs. Mayes who was sitting on her porch, "Ma'am, may I water my horse? I believe he is thirsty and would abide a moment's rest here in this pleasant shade."

"Of course," she said, having noted the rider's black jacket, white shirt, a black string tie in place, the reins in one hand, and a black book in the other hand. "Where are you bound, stranger?"

Her heart was telling her something. She just knew it. "Would you care for some lunch, sir? I'm sure I can rustle something up, or my daughter can. She's in the kitchen. Would you tell me your name so I can introduce you to her and my husband who is due here shortly?" She looked out across the grass and said, "Why, here he comes, and right on time."

"You are most hospitable, Ma'am. Most hospitable. I am Reverend Justin Dockery of the Gainful Ministry and we are looking for a place to settle into, possibly to build a church hereabouts in the future. We are not sure where."

The wedding took place in a week's time, Clarissa's father amazed by the speed and organizational capabilities of both his wife and daughter. Clarissa Mayes was married on the porch of her home, to the new sheriff of Winslow Hills, Travis Henry, whom she had been in love with for several years. Her mother said she was the most beautiful and happiest bride she had ever seen.

Over a hundred people attended the affair and a great time was had by all of them.

And later in the evening, after Reverend Justin Dockery said he had an appointment down the road and must depart, he and Gus Lamond spoke quietly near the barn.

"You did well, Jake," Lamond said. "You really carried it off. It's worth the hundred dollars. You did great. You don't have any bad feelings do you?"

"Not with the way that girl looked, Gus. She was a beautiful bride. I haven't seen one that beautiful in a long time. Besides, I made an oath to the Big Man Upstairs on the way in here. I promised I won't mess around again. We're okay on this."

"Well," Lamond said, "I guess you haven't been to too many weddings, have you?"

"No," said Gus Lamond's nephew. "I won't be in a hurry to do any more either. I had a hard time finding the book. The jacket and shirt and string tie were easy." He let out a soft laugh.

Lamond closed the night for the both of them, saying, "He's one of the new breed, Jake. I've watched him all the way. I guess you know that."

The both looked at Kid Bullet and his bride riding off to who knows where, the full moon in place, as well as love and a most welcome bit of connivance.

Linda Dove's Look-a-like

The West Roads Company stagecoach, on its regular run from Timkins Corner to Denver, was a half day late coming into the Pyburn Exchange Station, Jack Slack riding shotgun for Amos Leander. Slack had hurt his leg in a fall a few months earlier and was on the mend when Leander hired him to ride shotgun for a few trips.

"You can pick up a few bucks, a few free meals, and a few free drinks while you're still sitting on your butt," Leander said to Slack as they shared the end of the bar in Timkins Corner Saloon before the ride began.

"Ain't that a real bumpy run?" said a comfortable Slack as he sipped his drink, the coin in his pocket carrying less weight than yesterday, and him really conscious of being broke before he knew it.

"If you're afraid of a few bumps, you don't need or want the ride," Leander came back with, "but before I go I figure you owe me for the last round." He slipped that demand in as sly as a knife tip, knowing how bad the cut could get. "Besides, I'm pushing one of them new Concord stagecoaches right out of Concord, New Hampshire. You know where that is, don't cha, up north of Boston which is north of New York which ain't far from Washington. 'Sides, the rig runs like buttermilk all done up proper and is so smooth on one ride one of them gal passengers gave me a kiss at every station. She was all the way from Chicago and knew right where she was goin' all the time."

"Ya sold me, alright," Slack replied, "I'll take the job, and you buy the last round."

Leander smiled as he dropped the coin on the bar. "Two more, Jasper," he said to the bartender, "me and Jack's taking a ride 'cause I need a shotgun and Slim Debner's gone home for good, back to Chicago and 'enough of the wild land,' as he says."

The bartender said, "You won't miss old Slim you got Jackie boy here with you, but don't give him no shotgun, make it a repeater rifle. He's as good a shot as I know, but it ain't with no shotgun."

The new stagecoach, some of the shine still showing through the layer of road dust, and with only three passengers aboard, bound for Denver, topped the hill above Pyburn Exchange. Leander was getting the most out of his team as they tired near the end of their run and Slack kept his chatter at a quick pitch.

"It's like you said, Leander, smooth as buttermilk and I ain't bounced so little since I was on the Snake River with that Indian gal from Chimney Hill." While he talked he studied the small station in a clear area on the wide grass. He had not been at this station before and noticed many of the features of the layout; a small building for passengers' meals and where the station manager lived with his wife, smoke rising from the chimney, a corral that held almost a dozen big team horses, a man already running from the cabin to get a new team ready for the exchange and, in a bright red dress, a lady sitting on a bench out front of the station.

Slack immediately thought about the passengers in the stage and what a lady would do for the conversation, or for the awareness of all parties. One of them was a talkative drummer who had been this way before, as he heard him say on boarding the stage, "I am an old hand out this way. Been here a half dozen times and the ride has always been an uncomfortable one, but I swear, this trip got some cream on it." He was talking to a woman who was going to visit her son, "and he's the marshal of all Denver." She was a quaint but proud woman who was wide-eyed at most things that came new to her. Slack had heard her say, "My, oh my, everything out here is so big and wide and seems to go on forever."

The third passenger was a slick-looking gent, well-dressed in a never-seen suit, wore black dress gloves the whole trip, as if he was afraid to touch anything or anyone in the stagecoach, which made Slack think the man's outlook might change because of the lady in red sitting out front of the exchange station. And the closer the team came to the station, the more Slack saw that the woman would be a most welcome change for crew and passengers. When the coach stopped in front of the station building, the woman looked up at Slack who was staring down at her.

She did not seem to notice him staring at her, and turned and looked away, out across the prairie.

But Slack thought that for a bare second their eyes had locked, that there was recognition in some manner, at some level. He was not sure.

The lady in the red dress kept to her seat as the station manager, Harry Lampler, came around from the back of the building with the replacement team. He yelled to Leander, "Amos, I'm glad to see you. That rig still smooth as last trip? I don't know if you're late on your run or early for tomorrow." He was a big burly fellow with a wide grin and a chuckle in his throat any time he spoke.

Leander joined in his levity. "You know I ain't no later than usual, Harry, and never ahead of any schedule. Not with the horses I get from you gents on the trail. Sour Schmidt said hello to you and the Mrs. on our last stop."

"You know he don't mean it, Amos," Lampler said. "He ain't made for any kind words. Been that way f'ever." He looked over his shoulder at the lady sitting on the bench and said. "I got another passenger for you if you're moving on this late; name's Sandra Toner. She came up in a cart with a gent last night and he just dropped her off. Didn't say a word and she ain't said none neither, but she's a looker, ain't she?" He looked at Slack and said, "Who's your new gun slinger? I ain't seen him before, but he looks like he seen her before the way he's staring at her and her at him part times. You know her, son?"

"Naw," said Slack, looking off to the prairie. "I just thought she looked like a lady I saw once, name of Linda Dove." Many people heard of Linda Dove, though some may not have admitted it; she was supposed to be the most beautiful "house mother" in the entire region west of the Mississippi.

The lady in red, who called herself Sandra Toner, did not move an inch or a muscle when Slack said the look-alike name. She continued to look west, as if she was seeing a part of Denver that she'd soon get to, had been waiting to see. But all the people at the station had noticed her beauty, her regal air and the quality of her attire; she presented a most lovely picture of a woman, made more acute by the crude surroundings of the Pyburn Exchange Station, the open west at its feet, the wild west here for the mere looking.

The wondering and the curiosity mounted in the three working men, and soon worked on the three passengers as they entered the station building for a quick meal, all knowing they might have to spend an evening in the vast middle of nowhere.

The decision was made by Amos Leander and Harry Lampler that they'd best stay at Pyburn Exchange for the night and start out at daybreak. Both Slack and Lampler kept eyeing Sandra Toner, unable to take their eyes off the beautiful woman, and Lampler's wife laughing at him half the night about his "crazy dreams in the back half of his life." He laughed with her.

It was Slack who penetrated Sandra Toner's careful reserve, not aloofness but a want to remain separated as much as possible. Slack interpreted that to mean she did not want to talk or have to present alibis or stories about her current travel plans. He made it a point to talk about other things as soon as he determined that she had interests other than what her appearance gave off.

"She's a real good cook, isn't she?" he said to Sandra after Lampler's wife had fed them, a meal which she seemed to whisk up in a hurry after their late arrival.

Sandra responded, "I always wished I could cook like that, like my mother used to cook."

"Where was that?" he said, a smile on his face as if he was remembering his mother's cooking at the same time.

"Oh, back in New Hampshire, in a small town called Crowd's Rush, before my father moved us out this way. He was chasing gold and never found it."

"I never heard of no Crowd's Rush," he said honestly, and she laughed the break-in easy laugh and said, "Neither did I. I was just checking your honesty."

Both of them had a nice laugh and were comfortable with each other.

"I hope you find what you're looking for," Slack said, looking off as if he too had someplace to head to.

It did not take much more of his sensitive approach to hear what was in her short history.

In explanation Sandra Toner said, "A really bad man named Slade Briskom said he was going to kill me and my brother, for a simple slight, which I can't even remember now. I didn't believe him, but when my brother was shot down in the middle of the night, at close range right in the back, I left town. I fled to my former husband's place in Chandler Valley." Her head shook in disbelief, and condemnation.

She paused there and Slack figured she was trying to decide if she should continue.

The answer came shortly, when a soft look crossed her face as she studied him and saw his real concern. "I'd been married to him only for two years and he ran off. He remarried and had twin babies and wanted nothing to do with me anymore. Said it should be easy for me to understand how he feels because I couldn't give him any children, so he agreed he'd ride me out here so I could get a stage and not have to go into any town and get noticed. He said that word would be sent on to Briskom wherever he was and he'd chase me to the High Sierras on a chance he'd catch me, and anybody with me. I know that man that well."

Slack, disarmed by her plight, said, "I'm sorry you had to run into two men like that. You sure deserve better. I would guess you are the loveliest woman I've ever seen, and that includes the woman I saw who I really thought was Linda Dove."

"Where did you meet her, Jack?" she said, her hand touching his with a sense of humor, "back along the way?"

He blushed, "Yes, Ma'am, back along the way." But he found a sudden brazenness to say, "I'm glad it wasn't you and I'd sure like to get you to where you want to go, if I can."

She said, softly so nobody would hear her, "I'm in your hands, Jack." She touched one of his hands again.

In the early morning, as the team started out on the next leg of the journey, dawn unwrapping around the Pyburn Exchange and all the way out to the far peaks of a high rocky range, the last star sitting at the edge of one of the high peaks, distance finding its way into a coyote call so far off it came lonely and measureless, Leander said to Slack, "You sure had some vittles to fit you this morning, Jack. You got more energy than any man laid up with a bad leg than I've seen in some time, Yes, siree, Bub."

He clapped Slack on the back. "I can't wait to get home either, Jack." He roared with laughter, as the team picked up speed, the coach truly floating on the road.

But even with their early start out into the wide expanses of the west, Slade Briskom was not out of the picture, and not far behind them, as it turned out in short order.

Slack kept hearing some of the other information that Sandra had given him about Briskom. "He has many friends, or so-called friends, those men who are afraid of him, afraid of their lives and the lives of their families. He's a killer, and if he ever finds out I am here in this station, he'll get here quicker than you can imagine."

He kept looking back over the trail from Pyburn Exchange, until Leander said, "Jack, we already been back there. Keep looking up front of us, that's where trouble's most likely coming from if it's coming at all."

The stagecoach was about two hours out of Pyburn when Slack saw a rider behind them coming across a wide stretch of the road more than a mile back, dust flying up around him and his mount. Quick thoughts flipped through his mind, most of them loaded with certain attributes of Slade Briskom that Sandra had told him, about his way in the world, his way with people, his way with a gun.

He scanned the trail out ahead of them and suddenly turned to Leander and said, "Amos, we got company coming up on us awful fast, and he ain't going to be nice company. I know that for a fact. When you get over this rise up ahead of us, slow the team down and I'll jump off and sit waiting on him."

"You'll break your fool leg, Jack. Bust it all to hell."

"It's better than all of us dead, Amos."

"Is it something to do with your new lady friend?"

"Yep, it sure is, and she's scared to death, as I am, and you ought to be. When I get off, you get going but not runaway style. I'll have my rifle with me and I want to come up on him from the backside."

Amos Leander, just over the slight rise, the silhouette of the coach hidden from the oncoming rider, slowed the team to a slow trot. Jack Slack jumped off with rifle in hand and quickly ducked behind a small rock formation. When he gave Leander an okay wave, he flicked the team onward.

It happened as fast as anyone can imagine: Slack heard the rider pounding on the trail behind him, and then abreast of him. From behind the rock formation he got a look at the man in the saddle, a pistol in hand, a look of death about his whole person as if the devil himself had taken over his body. There was no doubt in his mind it was the one person meaning the most harm to Sandra Toner, the love of his life, and whose life now and surely depended on him and his wits, his shooting skill, his prayers already in motion.

Briskom, up ahead of Slack, had stopped the team, his gun in hand and waving it around. Apparently ready to shoot anyone of them who did not do as he'd say.

Slack saw Amos Leander toss down his rifle, then three weapons flew out of the coach door that had swung open at Briskom's loud command. Slack was now walking toward the coach with a slight limp but with his rifle at his shoulder, his eye ready to settle on the sight at the tip of the gun barrel.

Briskom, not looking once around the area, his eyes locked onto the stagecoach door, waited for the passengers to step down out of the coach. The drummer came first, his hands in the air, then the gent still wearing black dress gloves, and he was followed by the mother of the Denver marshal "sure that all this would be taken care of."

Slack could hear her words clearly on the gentle breeze. He heard the horses nicker at their rest.

In her red dress, startled, looking around for Jack Slack and not seeing him, Sandra Toner stepped down from the coach. She looked up at Briskom, who looked down at her and said, "Well, Lady, I caught up with you just like I said I would. Who brung you to Pyburn? Tell me now so I can get him and give him what he plain deserves, after I take care of you like I said I would, and all these other folks who's interruptin' my day."

The cool lady in the red dress, not moving a muscle, not saying a word, trying to save who was trying to save her and all the others, saw Jack Slack, still with a limp, coming up behind Briskom, a rifle at the ready in his hands.

She said nothing. She did not take a breath.

It was the Denver marshal's mother who said, loudly and clearly, as she looked back down the trail at Jack Slack coming toward them, "I knew someone would take care of this situation." She was about to point at Slack as she stared at him, when Sandra Toner said, "Keep your mouth shut, lady."

Briskom, twice alarmed, spun around as he still sat high in the saddle. He swung his gun about, as Jack Slack, knowing he had perhaps but one shot at the killer, took aim, took his time as one bullet whizzed over his head, and killed the killer in his saddle as he was about to take another shot.

Sandra Toner rushed to Slack as he sat down in the dusty road, the reserve of strength in his leg finally letting go. She hugged him as he knelt in the dust, his smoking rifle beside him.

"Don't tell anybody I'm her," she said, "because I love you and want the best I can be for you without any surprises."

He leaned against her as he stood up. "Never a word," he said, "and I mean forever."

Amigo Juan's War

The argument didn't rage in the bunkhouse, but it seethed, a kettle on the hind end of a wood stove tossing off steam, the words now and then rising in like manner, slowly but surely and every once in a while the argument, or elements of it, came tinged with a taste of vindictiveness. Speedo Tamiroff thought it exposed a long-muted hate that right now might be gathering speed, heading somewhere, possibly into the middle of the crew. His gut was roiling but he had made his pitch to the seven other cowpokes.

"'That's all damned wrong, my friend," Amigo Juan had said in reply to the disgruntled Tamiroff. "'You can't make a wrong all right all of a sudden,' my pa used to say. He also said, 'An inquisition becomes a revelation,' and when he was getting to the core of things he'd say, 'An I becomes an Us.' He believed it. Every word of it."

Through talking he might have been, but paused and went on with, "And reading was his great joy."

That pause was significant, as though measurement was necessary, part of the pitch he was about to make, his mind shaping the process. He'd be ready for them, one and all, and thought back over all he'd said, and simply added. "War is hell no matter what, no matter where you fight it, no matter against who, and the who, it sparks me to say, is somebody against our boss, against that old man up there in the main house."

He hoped he was not in the midst of indifference, realizing he'd always been different from the others ... trying so hard not to let go of the past and yet hold onto the present, the future. This country, this new world, was wide open, full of promise as far as a man could see, as far as a man could ride.

"If they're against the boss, if they're against this old man who treats us like sons, if they want his cattle, if they want this land of his that we're living on and working on, then they're against us. They want us out of here. And by God, they're not getting by me."

Amigo Juan shifted his weight, the way you've seen some boxers do, with a certain haughtiness caught in the spice of the movement, a derring-do carrying a voice of its own, like a look right in the eye coming on hard as a horseshoe kick. It was his natural way of bracing questions, making a statement a long step beyond the general talk of most bunk houses; rumors coming wide as the grass, gossip slippery as a hooked fish being banked, and rankling innuendos by the wagonload all over the town of Salvation Creek, the saloon, the barbershop, any place where all kinds of men gathered. They were seen by Amigo Juan as enemies, for they did not mumble what they meant. They were fully understood.

There was no two-way traffic about Juan Amigo. Recently he had begun settling matters in the bunkhouse where no one else spoke up against any bully with power in his back pocket. Some had said it was a tough enough task for anyone "but extra hard for a gaucho from the pampas, 'the gent with the funny clothes.'"

The fact is, Juan Amigo was the first gaucho ever to drive cattle for Hughes Anderson in Utah, and old and sickly Anderson seemed about to pass on his holdings, The Swedish Dream ranch spreading over 40,000 acres of foothill brush, Salvation Creek itself slipping out of the mountains in several points, merging for a flow alongside the luxurious grass he'd grazed his cattle on for more than 20 years.

To stir the pot, not a single member of his family was left from the early days. He was a kind, lonely old man who owned a grand piece of real estate. It salivated some very ordinary men, and also all who knew about it and were not ordinary men.

There were secret jostlings going on in the background that most people, including Anderson himself, were aware of because the secrecy was not of any importance to those taking aim at his property. Included in the opposition side were two extreme groups in their plans; one was willing to wait for Anderson to die, by accident or by natural cause, either apparently on the old man's horizon the way he went at life; and the other side of that stance was about to make a move to hasten his death and hurry the impending acquisition.

The one grace in this plight was the high admiration old Anderson felt toward the young man from South America, like a bright light on horseback every time he saw him working a herd, tending to his horse, minding his manners as though he had been educated in the finest schools. Yet the only schooling in his background was obviously that which he'd learned on the wide grass of the pampas and added to here in western America growing by leaps and bounds through exposure to people arriving from all over the world. Some of those places were farther away than his pampas.

Anderson once observed, "Amigo Juan learns more of the trades and less of the tricks of newcomers crossing the territories in wagon trains. He's got an eye for it. He's a student of people."

Special Amigo Juan was, and different from any man who had ever worked for him, bar none. Anderson had picked up a good deal of the Spanish from his wife as well as from a number of hands he had hired over the years. He found nothing strange at all in calling him by the name he had given in introducing himself, the tall, wide sombrero in place (often changing it for a small derby-like affair, also making a statement of origin), the large curved knife (*faucon*) stuck in the back of his belt, the belt also holding a lasso and three-balled bolas for near instant hobbling of a target or an enemy. His loose trousers were distinctive, along with a *chirpo* or wrap-around and its accompanying poncho worn for weather protection. An artist would certainly, and with relish, paint him different from other cowpokes ... the outcome also being a stick-out on a horse; he could ride like the devil himself.

On the prairie he was auspicious; in towns along the way he was looked at as invader, wet-back, odd-lot, stranger from far off, an awed oddity in the funny hat or funny pants or a scary knife near at hand saying hand fights were gambles against a stacked deck.

He was auspicious, too, in the bunkhouse, by his speech, his phrasing. "A wrong becoming a right." "An inquisition becoming a revelation." "An I becoming an Us." Somewhat off-handedly, Amigo Juan had spoken words he'd carried for years, the very annunciation and subsequent echoes being part of his precious memory. Now they were getting up to speed, being used for the first time in a long span of driving cattle across dry grass, endless miles of it, eating grub he'd hardly favor come his choice, hearing the taunts from dozens of drovers. And the meanest and vilest from one drover in particular who bragged about killing unwanted men, useless people in his judgment.

Shove Dexter, talking about Juan Amigo's long haul up from the lower continent, said, "Hell, man, his back's wetter than that Injun we tossed over the falls at Break Bone Ridge one time, him too coming from another world of silly hats and silly tricks."

Amigo Juan knocked him totally hither with one punch, neither man carrying a weapon in the bunkhouse and Anderson gone to town in a buggy, unable to mount and comfortably ride a horse anymore. And he didn't bother to wear his gun belt or carry a rifle; an easy touch for any skunk met on a lonely stretch of the road or a bushwhacker.

The old man didn't last long on his own; in fact, he didn't get to town, a bushwhacker's slug catching him in the back as the buggy traveled over the rough stretch of road about two miles from that destination; the echo of the single shot fading in the grass.

A passerby heard the shot and investigated. He found the old man dead and raced to the ranch to tell the hands. Amigo Juan, already mounted, rushed not to the scene of the murder, but into town, getting a place at the end of the bar, out of sight on new entrants. He kept a steady eye on everybody who came in, where they went in the saloon, who they spoke to, who they huddled with if they huddled.

Of seven more customers who entered the saloon after him, he made particular note of two of them; one was a cousin to Shove Dexter, a mealy-mouthed gabber and rough-house like his cousin, one side of his face ever-reddened by a pot of scalding water a woman had hurled into his leering face in self-defense. His name was Host Dexter and if a man was ever misnamed it was him, because the livid red scar traveled down beside his left ear and came to a knotted end where his jaw exhibited an uncomfortable lump. The travesty of the scar gave the cousin not a sympathetic and curious presentation, but a hideous look. Amigo Juan thought it would be difficult to sit with the scarred man at a table and enjoy an evening beer; tales often told but not spoken. For now, this Dexter sat alone, spared of company, a loner.

The second man made note of, and so marked, was a stranger, wearing the dingy remnants of a Stetson and worn drover clothes as if he'd just left the saddle after a drive of many months. Everything about him appeared to be on its last legs, worn to the nub, tattered or in ruins. The only saving element to his appearance was an apparent morning shave and his shiny gun belt, the belt carrying a pair of pistols with wear-clean, bone-white handle grips. Immediately on entrance he sat himself at a table with two other men as though he'd been expected to bring news of a late journey or escapade, the men waiting with impatience filling their inquisitive looks. The two men at the table were cowpokes who worked at a spread up the valley and Anderson's favored hand recognized them right away.

Amigo Juan had never see this other man before, of that he was sure not only because of his state of dress, but the man's coal-black, deeply-set eyes looked back at him loaded with danger and all kinds of Hell waiting for ignition, the man obviously recognizing Amigo Juan from some quick description uttered at the table. This, Amigo Juan concluded, was an enemy, not only for him but for Mr. Anderson in a very recent past ... only proof at the moment lacking for the hangman's knot, or a quick, clean shot face to face or a bolo wrap about his thick neck.

Amigo Juan wished for dialogue to accompany his thoughts, set the scene as it was developing in his mind. And it was often that he was able to fill in gaps of knowledge with an intuition that grasped him with suddenness, and unwitting accuracy. He could smell danger, secrecy, murder, back-shooting, as if each insidious deployment had just been skinned of its outer covering, like a pungent lime that he had not smelled in years, an acidic taste sitting in his throat.

The silence in the saloon bothered him. Then he wondered what last word or words Mr. Anderson had muttered, something besides "Oh" or "What's that?" or "Amigo Juan, where are you?" Maybe he said, "I recognize the man standing over me, making sure I'm dead. I must keep my eyes still and open, stare at the sky, crook my finger under my leg like it's on the trigger. Maybe write a word in road dust that describes this bushwhacker, pin on him to a characteristic mark, one that Amigo Juan will recognize, for nobody else but him will pursue this death of mine. Perhaps, perhaps, I have already passed here."

The sensations of sound, imaginative and created sound, came upon Amigo Juan with considerable force. Once, a long time in the past, he had heard the wind sitting in the bottled end of a canyon catching the wind and tossing words at him that had no recall once they faded away. Warnings, he realized, were like that, minute alerts that heeded observation, understanding, reaction.

In a boisterous blast from youthful days, came the yells and howls of his friends as they raced on the pampas; *"Así se hace, Victor." "Gran tiro, Juan." "Carmín, el gran vaquero."* ("Way to go, Victor." "Great shot, Juan." "Carmine, the great *vaquero.*"), the *boladeros* whistling in the wind, the hoof beats like drums from a near jungle of trees and the mysteries, the elusive joys that he knew would never come again in the same sounds, would never bring the same feeling. But he knew he'd have gone back if it hadn't been for the friendship and love for the old man shot dead in the road dust, but surely by now brought home by some of the hired hands. There'd be hell to pay if he hadn't been taken care of; and now it was his turn, his piece of the war someone had started from the depth of Hell and one old man the lone target.

This other yell coming at him was different ... no joy in it ... coming across the otherwise sudden silence in the saloon, gravelly, guttural, full of vitriol and hate and bigotry: "Hey, you, you sod Americano from Sod America. How come you keep starin' at me? What's this new crap of yours have to do with me? I just came into the saloon for a drink and you keep starin' at me. What you got goin' on me, huh?"

"I heard this minute the echo of a single bullet. One shot from a coward's place of hiding. One single echo of an old man dying at the single shot of a coward shooting from the darkness of trailside trees or a big boulder, or from behind a log big as a dead mule. One echo that traveled all the way from the west road to town and ending up right here in this room."

"Well, well, well, the Sod Americano's got something to say about someone dying. Is that it, Amigo? Is that it, Sod Americano? You sayin' I killed some old man who couldn't even take care of himself?"

Amigo Juan stepped away from the bar. "I didn't say anything about an *old* man. How did you know an *old* man died, if you weren't out there?"

"Oh," came the reply. "My friends here told me."

"You're a liar, *señor*. They were here when I got here and I came right from the dead man, the old man with the bullet in his back, and then you came in, and those two pals of yours better get away from the table because I'm coming over there to smell both of your pistols to see if either one has been fired in the last hour, or *aproximadamente*. And before you die you're going to tell all of us who hired you to bushwhack an old man who sold his ranch to me a month ago."

The two men at the table, suddenly aware their plan had caused a useless death, started to slide their chairs away from the table. One said, "We got nothin' to do with you, Grayson. Nothin' at all."

Grayson's fist slammed down on the table. "You two sit still and don't move. I'll talk to you after I finish all my business. I think your war has started already, just the way you wanted it, by Jingo. You think you're gonna own half the world out here before you die, huh? Better think again, the pair of you eggheads. If I go down, you go down with me." His face was drained of color, as if his blood had run away from him, filling his boots.

As cool as any *vaquero* ever spoke, Amigo Juan said, "None of you have it that cut and dry, Grayson," defiance exhibited in spades once more.

"It's my war now." Again he amplified his voice, the softness departed from it, a new hardness in its tone, "and you are going to have a piece of it. You'll be the second victim in this war, if the other two there at the table will kindly step aside."

His hand waved its warning.

It was an opening not to be ignored. He motioned to the two men who'd cooked up the murder scheme, flipping one hand against the *boladeros* swinging at his belt, the sound a threatening hollow issue, promising personal danger. There came announcements with that move, stories, pampas tales, *vaquero* mysteries afoot.

From half a world away, in an otherwise silent room, new circumstances had arrived at Salvation Creek.

"Believe this one thing before you die, Grayson," Amigo Juan said, letting the words slide through his lips with little moisture and just above a whisper, like Hell itself had stepped out on a sly move.

But the whisper penetrated all ears.

"Death is not easy by any means," he continued. "Often it is not quick like a bullet slamming its way through the chambers of your heart, or it is not explosive inside the head like cannon-ware or a foul grenade. It can be as ugly as venom, and as slow ... as slow as clotted blood in the last vein available. It can curse its half-way grasp on the breath like the hangman's noose without your feet taking a single step in death's final dance."

His body shook in a rhythmic and related gesture. At his side, in another move to instill fright and the full awareness of danger, he maneuvered the rawhide-wrapped *boladeros* with slick finesse; he'd brought that weapon from Argentina as though it was part of his person. It looked nothing more than a simple trio of leather balls attached to a braided set of leather cords. But most of the cowpunchers in the saloon had seen this weapon in action, taking down a horse, or a wild bull or a runaway target, or, without harmful intent, taking down squaw pine limbs off a dead tree for a campsite fire, the soft whir and whistle as they cut the air, and old Anderson once saying, "It was sure like blowin' on the embers of a fire before the flames came to light."

It was easy to see that Amigo Juan was transparent in all his motions, all his threats. As messages they could be seen, felt, almost tossing into the room the real smell of slow death. Here he was once more the true gaucho wrapped in honest conviction, in loyalty, with speedy and accurate use of pistol and *boladeros* and an imagination borne from the fields of home ringed by dark jungles. Those jungles, word had spread, were peopled by native tribes specializing in the darkest tortures. The stories he'd told around dozens of campfires raised the hair on the necks of many tough cowpokes, and even chilled a few of them with exaggerated fear. In truth, he was an odd danger to behold, on the wide prairie, in the confines of a saloon, and especially in the eyes of lesser men. Reputation as well as concord moved about with the man.

One of those lesser men was Grayson, for a moment frozen in place, his heart holding back on him, his breath too. This other man, the foreigner, was in command of the saloon, not himself as he had envisioned so many times. His eyes searching the room for support found nothing; not a raised eyebrow, not a wink of a sly eye, not the beginning sneer at the corners of a pair of lips, not a slow hand settling down on a side arm ready for wild commotion. The saloon stood as still as windless grass out on the vast prairie, hushed, not a single flicker of a blade.

He was alone ... at the end of the trail, against the stone wall of a last stand, catching what breath wavered in the room. His heart pumped too loudly, he thought, and the Stetson fell backwards from its perch on his head, the drawstring holding against a taught throat, a breath suspended at that juncture. His hand, too shaky to dare a quick draw, to ask for death at the hands of a damned foreigner, remained in place; judgment trying to exert itself, good sense.

It didn't help him, that unstable feeling. He struggled to compete, to stand up to the cowboy from another country, another world. And in that split second of judgment, of disbelief and wonder at the same time, his boots immovable, he knew he was servile in front of this man. He was beaten at his own game, his fingertips telling him so, the nervy lengths of his arms, his boots floating like loose stirrups, signals moving up and down his back as swiftly as clarions or the blast of a bugle.

None of it in his favor.

Slowly, still shaking, Grayson moved his hands, one at a time, to the buckle on his gun belt. His head was down, as though all the years told him he was going to end up this way ... like his mother had told him a hundred times or more, "Perhaps you'll be as dead as a log at the hand of a faster gun ... there's always a faster gun in the crowd, Sonny."

That wisdom was attendant again around Amigo Juan, new land owner in the new world.

The Horseman of the Davidos

Legends begin in strange settings with strange characters in strange times. This was such a story, in the shadows of The Davidos, where it began and where it ended on a very mysterious note.

And it was a time when the west was wild and wooly; sheep wars raged, stagecoaches and banks in small towns were objects of quick riches in the minds of scattered gangs, murder became commonplace in saloons at the drop of an ace of spades not fitting the deck, and out of the Davidos Mountain Range, in the Utah shadows, a black clad horseman, a single horseman, came off the rocky skyline and thwarted a series of holdups, robberies and thefts of all magnitudes. In a short time, the way legends move at breakneck speed, he became the dream of maids and maidens, the envy of sheriffs and marshals of the territory, and the figure young boys imagined when they looked down-range on their future.

A hero had arrived in the wild and wooly times and became known far and wide as The Horseman of The Davidos, a special man from a special place. The Davidos, for those who had not set eyes on the area, sat as pretty as any range of mountains, not at all as huge and terrifying as the Rockies, but a minor edition of a lovely but rugged setting on the edge of a most pleasant run of rich grassland for a hundred miles or so, between two grand rivers that more northern ranges had birthed.

The single horseman, riding a huge black stallion he called "Beau," wearing black garb head to foot including the mask hiding just enough of his face to deter recognition, firing two black-handled pistols unerring in accuracy, always appeared on the scene as if he had been created on the spot for the purpose of rescue and salvation for young maidens, old men and much money.

His sense of timing was so provident that he was said to have the ear of the Almighty One looking down from the Mountain of Creation, a name given by local Indians. Men of deep imagination said the Indians in time would come up with a better name, once the word spread among them that the horseman favored no man, no tribe and no nation except those subject to unlawful alarm, trepidation, outright danger and, on certain occasions where plans went awry, death and mayhem.

At the ninth or tenth rescue of coach passengers on the Bellville-Campasa Road alone, brigands scattered to the winds or slain by the single horseman heedless of his own person, the word about the new hero leaped from town to town, ranch to ranch. In turn, the entire Davidos Range was invigorated by the claims of witnesses about the mysterious horseman, regardless of several claims appearing to be inflated, as timing said they happened on opposite ends of the road at the same hour of the same day.

He could not be in both places at one time ... it was said ... unless there was more than one of him.

In Campasa, at the council meeting of elders, the meeting held in the rear section of the saloon with the bar closed temporarily, the talk kept coming back to the horseman clad in black garb who had thwarted the known hold-up attempts and more as the whispers and rumors spread and fed on themselves.

Rex Morgan, the blind rancher who had lost his eyesight to such a group of roadmen five years earlier, led the conversation back to the strange savior each time the topic seemed to switch around.

"Whoa, here. Dammit, whoa," Morgan would say, in his demanding voice, an operatic tenor at command. "What's going on here? I thought we were talking about this unknown hero, this gent in black, and suddenly, like dinner came on the table, someone wants to talk about the price of cow meat. Money won't mean a damned thing if the robbers keep hitting the stages, the banks, the mine deliveries. One man can't be everyplace at once. We got to set some rules here. If we find out who he is, do we make him marshal of the territory?"

His eyeless gaze went around the room, face to face, eye to eye, in a display of mysterious intensity, as if he was actually seeing each face and peering into each mind, the way it was said he declared his intentions to the soldiers under his command in the war.

"Do we give this gent a posse to run the bad guys aground? A big posse? An army of a posse? I say 'Whoa, robbers' when I think of him in command of a militia. We have problems in our lap that one man is facing down. I want answers plain and simple. For all we know them gents doing these deeds, or trying to, have set their eyes on our bank as a new target just as we sit here and talk about it. Wouldn't surprise me one tail feather. They're human like us, and they grow and get better at what they do, or they fall back and finally disappear. I'm not waiting for them to disappear, and I want to know who is or who ain't. Looks like they got trouble with this strange gent, but not from us, least the last time I looked. Let's get together on it for once and for all."

Morgan's story was known, if only transparent a bit, by all the council and those citizens who sat on the side. The upshot of it all, behind his bravado, was that Morgan kept hidden some element of the accident that caused his blindness, which he had never revealed to any other person, as if he alone on this good earth was to make amends, even in his blind state: he would see justice done, reparations made, vengeance accounted. The secret would stay with him until resolution.

He was a man of his word, just as the horseman from The Davidos was to his mission. Any new man in town, looking on Morgan, would find certain parts of the man coming back at him in a strong manner. They would be his sense of directness, his perseverance of task, an innate muscular power that remained about his person in spite of blindness, and the ready grin or grimace called up from down around his toes by which he was able to diffuse people when he wanted a discussion turned his way, diverted or changed.

The merchant of the group, Toll Brandon, with heavy investment in inventory for the territory, averse to any and all challenges except those he could read all the way from the start, like sure things, stepped into the argument, standing for attention the way an orator sets his stance or the Sunday preacher making the point of his sermon.

"Rex," he said, "I go along with what you say, but don't you think we should expend some effort in finding out who this gent is? Put a bird dog on the job? I'll put in some of the money. Have the bird dog start searching The Davidos for the man's place of operation? He has to hide out up there in the rocks. He found it, why can't others? A hideout is just that, a place to rest between operations. If it's not a cave or an old mine, it's visible from someplace else, from higher ground, from an old trail. Mountain men been traipsing up in there for more than 50 years I reckon. To a trained eye there shouldn't be any surprises."

He had made his entry and passed through. His gaze also went around the room, seeking acceptance, acknowledgment, never knowing the blind man in front of him could see every move he made, every change in stance, his total presentation.

Morgan, keen as ever, understood the merchant, and did not like him for a variety of reasons. But this revelation came strongest knowing that the merchant had made a verbal stance, had made himself "active" in the barest sense, reading it in the man's voice. Morgan had been able to do that since his first day of command in the army of the Potomac; it had become habit with him. He had a keen ear that had gotten keener at all levels since his loss of sight re-established the old saying that the blind get keener with other senses. He trusted his readings, swore he could smell cowardice or duplicity.

Two days later, with services ongoing in the Campasa Church of the Favored God, an excited rider dismounted at the church and hustled to Sheriff Bean Calder who sat right inside the door of the church. "He did it again, Sheriff, drove off some masked men trying to take the stage due here this morning. Two folks are being tended outside town at the B-Box-B Ranch, two robbers are dead, and three others broke off and ran. The Horseman from The Davidos did it again. Then headed up into the mountains like he was following the runaways. Ain't he the wonder?" He looked around at the congregation, as if he wore a deputy's badge, and said, "Want me to round up a posse, Sheriff? We can chase them gents to ground if we get hot on their trail. Maybe this Davidos gent leaves us some markers on the trail. Wouldn't surprise me one bit."

Calder said, "Hold on, Baker. I'm waiting on the council to make up its mind."

"Hell," said the young man, "they been sitting on it for weeks. You don't expect them old bucks to do anything that gets them too excited do you?" He looked around at the congregation as he understood what he had just said in front of all those in the church. He saw a few red faces, a few hidden faces. He saw a smile fly across the face of Rex Morgan, the blind rancher. Morgan's thunderous "Amen," echoed in the corners of the church.

Calder, in his quick survey, saw that most town men and ranchers were at the services. He tried to remember later who did not fit into his picture. Who he remembered at first call were Toll Brandon, the merchant, an odd sort to begin with, one deputy who had a new girlfriend out on an outlying ranch, and two men from the stage line that had an office and a livery in town. Most other respectable men of town and local ranches came to services on a regular basis.

When services ended in a matter of minutes, all men including most of the town council gathered around Calder as he stood off to the side.

"Give me the word right now, gents, and I'll organize a 10-man posse and commission it for a week if need be. We hope the Davidos Horseman will leave some kind of trail as he follows those gang members who got away. The trail is barely a few hours old. We have a good shot this time." He seemed anxious and nervous, like a racer getting ready to compete.

There was murmuring, a bit of noise among the gathering, and then Morgan said, "You got 'em, Sheriff. We're all volunteers now, on town payroll if needed. It's been set by the quorum in attendance at this moment. You pick the ten men. You're the boss on this. Those who stay will make sure the necessary work is done for the men you pick for the posse, ranch-wise, cow-wise, whatever."

He shook Calder's hand as the sheriff began calling out names. There was no further discussion, and an hour later the posse headed out of town, bound for the trail up into The Davidos foothills, on the trail of The Horseman of The Davidos on the trail of desperadoes on the run.

Morgan and a few men headed from the church to the saloon, the minister with them. It was a Sunday ritual, right after the other ritual, offering thanks from one and all.

In his fashion, in his way, Morgan knew who was with them and who was not without asking a single question. He knew every voice, and could bring back a five-year old image of the man's face, provided he was not a newcomer to town. Satisfied with some things in his mind, and quizzical about others, Morgan departed the saloon and proceeded to the telegraph office. It was an easy walk for him, knowing the layout of the town.

"Hey, Jess," he said to the man operating the telegraph key and sending out a message. "You on all week again?"

"Rex, you amaze me the way you can read who's sending on the key. I saw your head cocked as you came around the corner. You knew it was me and not Desmond soon as you turned the corner, didn't you?" He put out the non-working hand and tapped Morgan on the wrist. "You found out early on that it was all on the wrist, from what I figure. And I also figure, it being Sunday and some of the boys washing the whole week out of their souls, that you have something else on your mind. But for the life of me, I can't figure that part. I guess I'm blind to that part." He chuckled a low laugh that Morgan counted on. "So what's on your mind, Rex?"

"I have to dig for some information, Jess, but I don't really know what I'm looking for. Maybe something out of the ordinary, like information on stage shipments, stage passengers, mine shipment deliveries, and who has been privy to that stuff, or, more important, who's been asking the same kind of questions that I am."

"Got to do with the masked horseman and the way he knows where the boogie men are? I have to think about that. Sometimes it's like an offhand question from somebody, and I just pump out the works. Yet, wait a minute. Hey," he said, "if he needed it, the gang needed it just as much."

"So, something working in that noggin of yours?"

"I'll tell you something, Rex. It concerns a couple of people that downright ain't on my favorite's list."

"That being Toll Brandon for one, Jess, and I'll let you have the other one as a surprise for me."

"Brandon's right. Seems to sneak information out of me without trying, but he has a lot of business by stage and wagon, so I never questioned that."

"Who else?"

"Sheriff Calder, for one, and that guy who packs iron for the freight agency, Burl Smithers. Calder's doing his job, I figure. Maybe the other guy, but he comes around regular, gabs a bit, spends an hour like he has a whole day to do nothing, and then he's out of here like he got hit in the ass, like he's been shot."

"Any of them make notes?" Morgan said.

"Just Brandon. Carries that work pad everywhere with him like his life depended on it. That enough for you, Rex?"

Morgan nodded, put one hand out that the telegrapher touched, and they parted without any more word exchange. And Morgan had more questions in his mind than when he entered the telegrapher's office.

Three days later, in the heat of evening, the posse came back to town, and every man headed straight for the saloon, but Calder and his deputy were not with them.

One posse member yelled out to the saloon owner, "The sheriff and his deputy will be in later, Harry. They're doing something at Morgan's place they said. He let us go after the fight up in the hills, after we got all the gang and brought three of them back. They're in the jail now, locked up tight."

The saloon owner said, "The Horseman of The Davidos lead the posse to them?"

"Damned right he did," the posse member said. Last I saw of him he was pointing down into a box canyon. They were hiding behind a rock fall, with their horses. That guy in black sat his big horse uphill of us, on the other side of the canyon. The bad boys were shooting at him. He might have been hit, but I'm not sure. Sheriff just said for us to hightail it back here and get wet on the town fathers.

There, an hour after arrival, Calder filled in Morgan with all the missing information, and in a backroom. He insisted on privacy.

"Hear me out, Rex. This is pretty hard to swallow, and it sure is a mixed up story, but I have to tell it my way. Please hold off until I'm done. Like I say, it's damned involved."

He paused, took a swig of beer, and then went right into it. He drew a piece of paper from his vest. "This is a bill of sale, with the owner's name signed and my signature as witness. All you have to do is sign it where I tell you. It's the bill of sale for all Toll Brandon's property. It's yours to do as you wish. Secondly, Toll Brandon is now buried on your ranch, in a far corner. His horse is corralled in that L-shaped canyon off the hills. The horse, too, now belongs to you, in a manner of speaking."

He took another swig of beer. "It's a big black. The black clothes that the horseman wore are now in safekeeping with your wife. We spent an hour with her today. She knows everything and it's all legit."

Morgan, catching an edge in the sheriff's voice, said, "There's a whopper here, Bean, that you're not telling me, like maybe Toll Brandon was the ringleader of the whole bunch."

"That ain't quite right, Rex. He was The Horseman of The Davidos, lock, stock and barrel, and he swore us to secrecy, you and me, as he lay dying in my arms. He knew he wasn't one of your favorites and he kept it that way. 'We've come a long ways,' he said, 'and we can't stop now. Have someone put on my clothes and become me. Pick a good and trusty man. Promise me. Get to Rex Morgan and tell him the same thing. Rex is a good man, even if he can't see it all.' He laughed his last laugh at that. 'Let The Horseman of the Davidos keep riding, keep after the bad guys. Let him ride forever. We need someone like him. If he gets killed, dies like what's about to happen to me, get someone to take his place. We'll all be better for it, especially me if I'm lucky enough to be looking down on you from the Mountain of Creation.' He closed his eyes then and was gone."

And so it was, thirty years later, when Rex Morgan was sick abed, Sheriff Calder long since dead, that Morgan told his wife, "Don't let any of our boys wear those clothes anymore, Ethel. Tell everybody that The Horseman of the Davidos died in the waters of one of the two rivers, his clothes beside the stream, his latest horse tethered nearby, and his body not to be found anywhere."

But The Horseman of The Davidos patrolled the road for all those thirty years along the Davidos range, like the legend he had become.

Yuma Tranquility

"Nothing's out there, boys, as far as you can see or ride in three days," said the jail keep of Yuma Territorial Prison as he locked the first iron gate behind Paulson and Newberry, convicted of robbing three banks in the territory, killing one teller, and another robbery, a botched one, in which two customers did not live past sundown.

Their short saga at robbery was known far and wide in the territory, and their trial was meat and potatoes for local papers all the way to St. Louis and Chicago. The two men could not cast more difference in their appearances than what came to the jailkeep's eyes right from the first. Hubie Newberry, meek and mild looking, with an innocence locked into his eyes, was a stark contrast to an up-and-at-'em type of scoundrel everybody saw in Russ Paulson... but not harsh or mean or with a killer instinct.

They had loudly protested their innocence before and after their trial, which was completed in short order.

When the jailkeep locked the second iron gate behind the pair, looking as heavy as if it would withstand the charge of a buffalo herd, bars thick as a man's wrist, he said, "This ain't the last one, boys, but it might as well be. Nobody ever got past this gate, not since I've been here, and I've been here forever, believe me. This is the Hell Hole of the west, of the universe, the hottest, driest place you'll ever know. You'll be sorry for every mistake you ever made while you're in here, behind these bars."

The third iron gate, thick as #2, slammed shut with a dull, solid, but resounding clang against the stone wall promising it could hold off the disbanded Army of the Potomac, if necessary.

From the outside of the gate, lighting his first cigar of the day, the jailkeep said, with an ominous tone in his words, "That one does it, boys. That's the end of the booze, the ladies, and the trailside campfires you probably grew up with. No music here. No shivarees. No fun. But lots of work on the rock pile so we can build another wall. This is the end of freedom for you famous bank robbers. But you ain't the only bank robbers worth knowing in here. There's more, believe me."

He walked off without a look back.

The sentence had started, for crimes they had not committed.

"None of it's fair, Russ," Hubie Newberry said to his saddle pard, Russ Paulson. "We didn't rob no bank. We didn't kill no old man and no old lady. We get all the blame for what somebody else did. What am I gonna do now, Russ? I can't stay in here. Already I can't breathe right. I feel like I'm gonna scream."

Paulson, know-it-all with conviction, experimenter in many things, who delved into what makes a man tick like a clock sometimes and gets all out of whack at another time, said, "Haven't I always taken care of you, Hubie? Always thought of you first? So, guess what I'm thinking of now."

"You tell me, Russ. Sometimes I know I'll never catch up to you. But this ain't out on the grass taking our time going anywhere we please, anytime we please, or some canyon where we can light a fire anytime we want. This is jail."

"Now, Hubie," Paulson said, waving his hand back and forth in front of Newberry's eyes like a fan was in it, his fingers open and falling shadow-like one after the other across his vision, "you sit back and think about me swinging my hand and you getting your mind all in one calm place outside of this jail and getting sleepy like you always do. There's no difference for us in here. They don't know it, none of them, and the big shot jailer thinking he scared us. Even he don't know what's coming, what we can do feeling the way we do, sleepy as all get-out, slow and calm and forgetting about jail and thinking all the time about being out on the grass and the horse under us in a slow trot and the stars coming out and a campfire coming up in a new place just over that next little mound of grass or over there in the shade of those cottonwoods sticking up like a bunch of arrows in a quiver, the ones you're seeing just about now, and we can go off to sleep under them thousand stars up there or maybe a chunk of the moon coming over the hill right behind us soft as a woman's shoulder."

Paulson paused, a sincere smile crossing his face, the jail disappearing from his own mind as Hubie Newberry, nodding his head, started into his usual trance.

"Don't you feel it now, Hubie? Like the grass is smooth as a buffalo robe, and warm and easy to sleep on, and those stars up there are winking at us all the time because they know what we know, all this secret stuff that that Shaman taught us in the mountains? Now it's our turn at all the secrets, Hubie, so rest easy. This jail is easy as falling off a log for us, and don't you wake up until I snap my fingers twice."

A wide and happy smile sat on Paulson's face as Newberry went into his hypnotic state; and just at that minute a guard walked to their cell door and said, "I heard a lot of crazy jabbering goin' on here, and now I see your pard's got himself to sleep in a hurry. Takes a crazy man to sleep in this place, so we ought to wake him up," and as he was about to rap a rod against the cell bars, Paulson put his waving hand up and said, "He's only dreaming of being out there on the grass and us having a nice campfire and a few stories and a few drinks and some company coming from town to help us get through the soft darkness and then all those prairie stars finding their way almost down on top of us as we go off to the same kind of prairie sleep that Hubie's having right now. That's an honest sleep that comes to men of good souls and kind hearts, like the heart you have, seeing that campfire and company from town and those stars calling down to us or practically falling in our lap some nights. Don't you agree to that? And you can stay calm and easy and I won't tell anyone, even the top jailer that you rested your eyes for a while, and you can't open them up until I snap my fingers one time."

Paulson nodded at the guard, asleep on his feet, the steel rod he carried down low at his side.

He said to the guard, "I'm going to ask you a few questions and you can tell me the answers if you want, but I won't tell anybody, even the top jailer. Is that okay with you?"

"Yes," the guard said, his eyes closed, his breathing unhurried and peaceful.

"When is the best time to walk right out of here, Mister Guard? When you're having your well-deserved rest after a hard day? And which way should we go when we quietly walk away without any trouble breaking out and no noise at all and nobody knowing we're gone until a whole bunch of hours later? And where would we get a couple of horses if we did decide to walk away and leave this place and leave you having this nice sleep that you need all the time?"

The guard, in a monotone, said, "Around midnight, after all the guards change over for the night, and they start their own on-duty night's sleep anywhere they can while the warden's sleeping and all the prisoners have given it up for the night. If you went northwest, your tracks would be harder to follow. And going that way you'd find the horses are about a half mile off, down in a gully where most of Yuma's mounts are corralled. The warden wants them out of sight as much as possible so the prisoners won't get any wild ideas. No man has ever escaped from Yuma."

He paused in his hypnotic state, and said, "Oh, there was one, but the warden says he died out on the desert, without a doubt. The warden's talked about it a hundred times. How Crackbak Mellon-Mellon's bones are out there getting real bleached in Arizona's sun. Been dead alone out there for a long while now. Was kind of a funny guy, singing all the time. Bet he sung himself to death."

Paulson snapped his fingers once and the guard said, "Is your pard still sleeping there?" He raised the rod, intending to make some noise.

Paulson, waving his hand, said, "He's not really sleeping, he's just napping," and he snapped his fingers twice, behind his back, and Hubie Newberry yawned and said, "What did you say, Russ?"

During the next week, both men on work details, Paulson watching how things began to pile up on his pard so he had to straighten him out. In the meantime he finally realized which guard he'd set up for their escape. He decided that the route through the kitchen and off the back storage wall was the best way and gave them an added start northwest, the jailer's horses with them, the wild, unknown region ahead of them.

"The right time would point itself out," he said to himself. He laughed at that, easy with his own humor, Newberry wondering what his pal was at again, carrying on with the kind of stuff he could not figure out, laughing half the time, even in jail.

That same evening, after chow made itself known, foul as ever, the top jailer came by their cell, sauntering in his manner.

"I see your friend is sleeping again," the jailer said. "I hear all he does at night is sleep, but they also tell me he works hard as anybody during the day, after a poor start on prison life. Looks like he's consigned himself to life behind bars. Keeps a man on his back all night, too, the hard work. Nobody gets away from here. They're too damned tired and I'll keep them that way. Don't you get any crazy dreams about going on any trip. It just doesn't happen here at Yuma."

Paulson wanted to have a go at the top jailer, but decided he didn't need the risk of the man being smarter than he appeared to be. Anyway, the joy would come once he and Hubie were out on the trail with the jailer's horses. That'd give the jailer something to talk about and try to go to sleep with every night from then on.

So he kept his hands clasped, his eyes down, in a show the top jailer would think about before he went off to sleep, and his mind echoing "another tough hombre taken in hand." Paulson remembered the old Indian shaman who told him he learned a lot from the wolf pack and their ways in the world, how a whole pack of them would almost bow to the leader of the pack.

Dawn came over Yuma the next morning like a gunshot, sunlight pouring in on the prisoners as they got ready for a day of work, some on the rock pile, some on yard clean-up, some at the small garden near the kitchen where a few hardy plants kept their heads above ground and their roots in place.

Paulson and Newberry were with the rock gang again, the top jailer moving them around, finding something odd with the two and not wanting them to get too familiar with certain details of the prison. Newberry, he noted, worked feverishly but didn't accomplish what Paulson did, with the same tools in the same time frame. That difference sat working in his mind, but he couldn't fathom any reason behind his observation except the handling of tools looked easier in the hands of some men. Perhaps part of it was actually an art. Some men, he noticed, had a swing and a rhythm in them that came out in their work. Now and then he remembered Crackbak Mellon-Mellon and how work was easy in his hands, tools had a grace with him, and the song was always on his lips regardless of how much it irked him, the top jailer.

So, after a hard day in the sun, after a meal as poor as usual, all the prisoners went back to their cells, letting sleep call on them. Night crawled into and through all the bars of the prison, making its statement to all the prisoners. The calm settled on many of the prisoners, sleep being the only answer to the problems beating at them.

Hubie Newberry slept as calm as always after a hard day's work. Paulson, alert, always on the watch for any edge, any useful information, waited for the right hour to come, for the right day was at hand. He could feel it in his bones, in the very air of his cell, in the slow breath of night advancing on Yuma its ultimate closure.

He woke Newberry up to tell him that they were leaving that night.

"Where are we going, Russ, if we get away from here?"

"We're going to see that Jed Hammond who told those lies about us. He will write an admission of his guilt, telling who put him up to it. We'll give that to Lloyd Wagner at the newspaper and let him use it. He's one honest man, at least."

"We won't have to come back here, Russ? Not ever again?"

"Never again, Hubie, if I can help it. So you have to do exactly as I tell you, right down to the minute, to the last detail."

"Are you sure I can do it, Russ? I don't have any idea of what's going on."

"It's a snap, Hubie. The skids are greased, have been for weeks and weeks. Don't worry about it."

At five minutes past one o'clock in the morning, at the cell of the two innocent men, Paulson hypnotized the guard, who gave them his keys and side arms and laid down in their cell to continue his sleep.

"You won't wake up, Tory," Paulson said to the guard, "even when the sun hits the high windows in the morning. And we'll be going southwest with all the speed we can instead of the way you think we'll be going." He patted the guard on the shoulder and left him on a bunk, closing the door behind him.

It was a cakewalk, he would say, as they used the guard's keys to get past two doors, slipped into the kitchen where not a soul was yet at work, and slipped over the wall at the back of the kitchen. The final wall, beyond the slop bins and sump dump, was managed in total darkness and near silence. Like sparse shadows, they slipped down the road and into the gulley where the horses were. They had their pick of the mounts, including saddles and full canteens, and two rifles scrounged from a tool room. They rode off as silently as ghosts, with two extra horses on lead lines.

No names were called out. Nobody got hurt. Not a shot was fired. At dawn that day, as the sun rose behind them, they were more than 40 miles away. They unsaddled their tired mounts and saddled the spare horses for the next stretch of the ride, and all four horses set out. They covered 200 miles in a circuitous route, and were northeast of San Diego, in a canyon, a fire lit, a meal in the offing, when they were attacked by a sheriff and two deputies.

Paulson shot two of the men right off their horses and Newberry got the other man.

"What'll we do now, Russ?" Newberry said, his face as sad as ever.

"We hightail it northeast tomorrow. If they catch us and send us back there, we'll know now that we belong there. We'd just do it all over again. Nobody but the injuns knows how we did it. That's our secret every time out."

And he gave off a little laugh that Hubie Newberry never caught up to.

Me and Tozzer

Me and Tozzer was lookin' to go to Canada, or at least Montana, which we called Montan, and know the Indians the way they ought to be knowed like face front and real as us. Course, we had some problems along the way, folks steppin' on our toes and their kids spittin' at us bein' us, but not them older folk, a black and a white kind of cowboy types. But we was quicker'n hell with pistols and gettin' them outta the holsters and lettin' loose and it showed I guess 'cause nary a soul really bothered us, 'ceptin' one big bear-mouth talkin' a whole streak o' nothin' right near the last camp we pitched in Ideeho under some pines and firs and had a nice fire goin' and he blows in like he's owned ever'thin' he's ever looked at, meanin' what was ours.

But they wasn't his no matter how he looked at them like they was and Tozzer sittin' back against a tree twice as big and round as me and him put together like it had been right there waitin' on him f'ever and the loud mouth makes pretend he's studyin' somethin' and he's all the time sneakin' his hand to get Tozzer's rifle and Tozzer noticed he had no rifle of his own so he just said, while he's just layin' against that tree comfortable like, "Don't," and loud mouth makes trick move to get it and Tozzer shot him before he even touched Tozzer's rifle, shot him right between the big loud mouth eyes like it was an extra eye for him, but bloody as a butcher's apron in a hotel kitchen, the kind you guess at 'cause you ain't ever been inside one, never mind et there.

Any way I got to tell you why we was goin' up to Montan in the first place, beside seein' the Indians, who was the real reason anyway. Only Tozzer liked them names they had for tribes, and he'd say them over and over so even I'd get sick of 'em, but he could say the same ones a hundred different ways like they was in a song, all them crazy but nice names that tickled him like his pappy used to, and they rolled out his mouth like words in a song ... Asssiniboine, Sioux, Crow, Blackfeet, Cheyenne, Kootenai, Salish, Shoshoni, Gros Ventre and Kalispel and probably more like they was all cousins of one kind or another and would have great parties when they got a together goin' for a celebration or a war all their own.

I was on the other end of the stick, wantin' to know how different they looked from one another in line or fishin' or huntin' and lookin' for the ladies who wasn't in their villages and not in them teepees either, the way ladies always has a certain way of thin's bein' what they ain't in the beginnin', if you catch my bait. I wondered aloud even to Tozzer as he sang them names how 8 or 9 or 10 of them in a row, with me studyin' them real close, could look any different from one to the next in line or the end of the line, and all wearin' feathers and skins and beads and wolf and bear teeth and bore tusks and whatever the get up was for a night out with ladies from one of them other tribes, if that was the way it was done up there in Montan with all them Nations of Indians, if such was it.

Of course, we seen a lot of them, and the stuff they was wearin' at special times and times not special, and Tozzer, way up when we was near some of them other territories and states and he learned some new names that plumb made his mouth go sweet with them, like Kiowa and Arapaho and Kansa and Otoe and Pawnee and Ponca and Lakota and Dakota Sioux and Arikara and Northern Paint and Palouse and Comanche and Pueblo and his eyes lit up at Apache and Bannock and Caddo like he was doin' a alphabet and then got so nice-soundin' for him 'cause of Nez Perce and Coeur d'Alene almost makin' him cry in his happy, and he'd sleep like a baby in the back of a wagon on a slow trip to wherever and them names comin' up in the night from his songs of all them Indian names.

That's my ridin' pard, Tozzer, said all the time his daddy was a king of a tribe down in Aferca or someplace on a ship. He was some mad, that boy, 'cause he never got to know any of them names from down there in Aferca, and I thought and never told him it was his own way of makin' all them names come good for him, 'cause I didn't want to spoil any of his fun and songs like he never once did say what was the difference in clothes they wore if they did besides skin and teeth of all kinds that once bit and chewed away at stuff, and all that bein' my fun of Indian thin's, like his was names.

Once a other time in Ideeho gettin' close to Montan where we was headed the whole trip, one of them tribesman stepped into the trail ahead of us like he was a spirit come loose from a rock of all thin's, 'cause that's where he was hidin' behind, and he holds his hand palm up like we seed before from other Indians and we know he's a friendly sort and he touched his face with his couple of fingers and points at Tozzer and we knowed he ain't never seen one of them Afercans before like Tozzer was, whose daddy or granddaddy was a king down there way off where a ship goes.

Tozzer picked that right up, as he's as smart as they come with folk havin' color in their skin and most like I thought had seen the question afore, so Tozzer touched his own face skin first and then reached to touch the other gent's face who steps back and whips up his spear and soon as breathe he's lookin' right down the barrel of Tozzer's pistol like it appeared outta the same hidden air the Indian came from, and he was a whole lot of surprise that red-faced Indian, who thought best to put down that spear of his and be nice to a gent who had skin almost like his on his own face. So, quick as he got that pistol ,out of his holster, Tozzer gets it back where it was, and they had smiles apiece them two with me lookin' on and appears he only wanted to touch Tozzer's black skin and then ask us for some whiskey which we had none of on that long trail to Montan or even past to the Canada.

But we had coffee with him of which he might have had afore and liked enough to empty our little firepot of dented tin. Then this redman wonderin' about a black man sat down and drew in the dirt a couple of peaks he pointed out for their realness and pointed his finger in between them he drawed on the map on the ground and shook his head and held his spear like he had throwed it a hundred times, and Tozzer said right off, "Well, Tug, 'cause that's what he called me all the time he wanted my attention, we ain't goin' up in there 'tween those two peaks 'cause we prob'ly ain't comin' out the other end." And Tozzer patted that Indian on the back like he was an old friend at a party and the Indian patted him back the same way and then the two of them in their own colors shook hands like we did at home and I swear it was the only time I ever saw red and black shake hands even in the middle of a rainbow, if you know what I mean.

I'm glad I made that trip with Tozzer ridin' beside me all the way, just like he was a rabbit's foot or a lucky charm from some snake lady back home or an old man so old his skin crawled in layers on his neck under his chin sayin' how old he was and smart and knowed thin's I never knowed 'bout charms and good luck pieces and poor dead rabbit's foot wonderin' if that rabbit ever made it to be a good meal or a stew for some hungry gent like we was sometimes on that trip until we got to Montan. All that way Tozzer was liked by all them tribes and he kept singin' them names and I gotta admit a couple of times that singin' a names got us a free way with some had us dead to rights with a lot more arrows ready to fly than we could shoot bullets back at 'em.

Thin' is all them red ones liked him and his face color and his long fingers so quick on gettin' his gun outta his holster and they saw the tricks he could do and it was like he was in a carnival for them, which they never had saw anyways I bet. They plain liked Tozzer like I did and we did get all the way to Montan as we had begun to call it and point out our way to all the Indians we met with them pretty names and after a lot of while I got so I could match a name with what a Indian was dressed up in, just like I had a name under a picture of him with skins and teeth on a string on his neck or what kinda moccasins he had made for himself outta a tough pelt or his woman did the makin'.

So we evened thin's out for Tozzzer and me and found a valley in Montan looked like what we thought heaven would look like when that time come to us down the trail someway, or up the trail as Tozzer was always sayin', knowin' we was headed there all the time.

This place we found 'cause another redman pointed it out for us, who prob'ly liked Tozzer as much as me, and it was perfect and had some wild horses in it and some cows got loosed from some herd and lots of good huntin' game for other meat food, and we built a lean-to at first we lived in 'til we made us a log cabin for just the two of us ridin' pards all the way up from Oklahom and other places, and one day we found a Indian girl with a broke leg on the grass and her horse dyin' after steppin' in a hole and throwin' her on top of a rock in the middle of the grass like it was planted there for her to break her leg on and we took her to our cabin for two which now was a cabin for three and she fell in love with Tozzer who fixed her leg for good and took extra care of her and I just had to get up early one mornin' and get outta there on my own and head for Canada places 'cause she loved Tozzer as much as me and him her.

One time later on I met a mountain man who knowed about Tozzer the black man with the redskin girl and they was friends of his and I sent a message to them sayin' I hoped they was happy still and the mountain man says they was happy and had a baby he saw only a few months past and it was as white as me and then he knowed why I left there in the first place but I was pretty sure he'd never tell anythin' to nobody.

But you knowed how that is I bet when one turns one way in a tight little space and someone else turns exact the same way and those little thin's can't be helped much from happenin'.

So I, Tug by name, send this to Tozzer my friend who can have all I left and ever owned just in case I get kilt out here, which might be my luck without my pal Tozzer and his foot off the lucky rabbit who must have been plumb unlucky in the beginnin' but got changed some.

Tug.

One Way to McAlister's, or Manitou's Tipi

"I'll tell you, son, that you can't go any higher than McAlister's in Colorado, and you'll go through hell to get there, and never on your own, never without some kind of map."

The oldest man in the room, in The Chauncy Remney Saloon and House of Good Taste and Better Scents, in the Colorado town of Munitions Mount, had the soap box and nobody was about to take it away from him. Some of them had waited, it seemed ages, for him to break down and say where he had been for a whole year when he was many years younger. Not one man ever heard a word out of him on the subject, but there had been signs in the last few days that a dent had been made, a chink found in his armor of silence. He was one of the two mysteries that had occurred in this section of the Rockies, but the mystery of where he had been that time was pale in comparison to the other mystery, the capture and eventual disappearance of a huge army ammunition train that had been taken in a night of ultra-darkness. In 20 years there had been no sign, word, or whisper about the fate of Captain Nathan Wexler and each and every one of his men on that assignment, bound to relieve Fort Dexter, under months of long siege by Indians.

The Chauncy Remney Saloon and House of Good Taste and Better Scents, sitting like an ink blot in a map of the area, was a piece of the Rockies that people on the east coast and the west coast and deep into Texas had heard about in every trail camp and western saloon for more than a thousand miles in some directions. Gone missing with the army munitions were the hundred men on the delivery mission bound for the foothills post of Fort Dexter, by this time, 20 years later, looking like not much more than rotting wood, a single flag pole bare of adornment, and so many stories that they could twist the hearts and minds of normal men. All listeners to awed tales of the area knew that The Chauncy Remney Saloon and House of Good Taste and Better Scents was both heaven and hell in a single wrapper, the ladies upstairs able to tell the most devious stories a man could imagine about the failed mission. Often those stories superseded the intended mission of visits upstairs.

All this was known by the old man who was doing the talking and whose name was Ship Hendry, Ship being no nickname but his regular born name, and was called by most folks as Mountain Tooth. He was a mystery to the day.

"You know what I think," one patron of the saloon said, "that he just said 'McAlister's' for the first time ever from his mouth. Never so much as whispered it afore, not him, not Mountain Tooth himself. First time ever, believe me, and I been here for all the years since the happening."

"I never heard of no McAlister's," said another gent about as old as the main talker who was keen enough to hear the whispers in the room.

"Its real name is Shipolo," Hendry said, "unless you want to call it the tipi of Kitcki Manitou or Gitche Manitou, whatever the Indians call him, but he's the Great Spirit, the one and only Great Spirit. That's the best I can fix it for you, and the old Indians say the only way to get there is a bridge up in them mountains called Ekutsihimmiyo, connecting here and there. Like heaven and earth can be connected, a bridge between Shipolo and Earth some of their elders say is near Mount Rainer up there in Washington close on Canada and others of 'em say it ain't real far from us as we sit here drinking up all this booze in the cradle of the mountains."

He looked out the large front window showing a view of white-topped peaks in the distance and lifted his empty glass in salute. One gent at the counter nodded at the bartender and another glass was at the speaker's elbow in a few seconds.

Hendry smiled his thanks at the bartender and then at the buyer, who just happened to be an acknowledged acquaintance of long standing.

Managing a laugh that could be interpreted many ways, Hendry said, "But I always called the place McAlister's 'cause that's the name of the real mountain man who told me about it, just like I'm telling you now. It's easier to say. You know I can't rightly say their name of the place or that confounded bridge that really ain't no bridge, but sure is a way to Manitou's Tipi, which is what Shipolo is, as I said. I ain't saying it's closer to earth or heaven but I'd've liked to have finished my days there, but it wasn't my calling to do so even though some of 'em when they found out my name was Ship took up a deep fondness for me."

A second old timer said, "You mean to tell me you been where White Fox has been talking about for years with all them ladies waiting to make new tribes to walk the whole earth?" White Fox was an old Indian who had come out of the mountains with endless stories and had become a "fort Indian" with few tribal ties.

"Well, now, I can't say what them ladies had for long-range plans, but I knew what made 'em giggle and call me Chief. And White Fox, from what I hear, ain't always throwing dust on the trail."

Most of the laughter came from older gents in the saloon, but one or two younger gents raised their eyebrows and simply pointed overhead to the second floor, and with a full and ready smile for those in the know.

"Well, Mountain Tooth, you ready to lead an expedition up to that McAlister's place, are you? Lots of us'd chip in for that long as we get to make our visit."

"You missed off what I said. There ain't no expedition, no bunch of mountain men or cowpokes or miners going to get up in there 'cause a bunch can't get in. It's too tight, too long, too dark, too set with smaller gods took up with weapons to protect the way. One man, with good direction, might slip in there like I did. But no partners. No pards of the saddle. No Mining diggers with all their gear. No plain old explorers looking for newness."

"So why're you telling us all this after all this time? Just making us itchy? Making the dream bigger than what it's been for a long time, too long? You got something else on your mind, Mountain Tooth? You ain't in possession of knowledge about Captain Drexler, are you? Or what happened to all his men? If nothing else, they ought to be buried if we could find them and their remains. That's only proper, ain't it?"

"I can't make it up there again, but I could give some younger man the right way to get there, tell him right up front how tough it's bound to be, and if he makes it, he won't get out of there for over a year."

For much of his talk, Hendry kept alert to a young man in the back of the room he had seen in action in a few situations, which aroused his curiosity and his commendation. The young man was Oren Bandley, part-time cowpoke, part-time miner on his own claim, but no hit yet.

Hendry had asked about the young man, and the livery owner said, "Bet a dollar on that kid any day in the week, Mountain Tooth, and you get it back plus some more. Works like a dog or a mule, no sass in his body, does what he's been told. My niece should have married him, but she's got the same luck I got and messed up already with the wrong one. Course, she'll never admit it."

It was enough for Hendry to go on, to bet on the Bandley boy, knowing he'd pay attention to all details, do what he was told, or at least do so to the best of his ability. "Ever see that boy in a tight corner?" made the livery owner smile in a hurry.

"Frisco Jimmy came in here one day, Mountain, and wanted only a paint and picked one out the boy just brought in for the lady he was working for. Frisco Jimmy says he wants the paint the boy has still got by the reins. 'He ain't for let or money,' the boy said, and Frisco comes back like he's in a corner and says, 'Know who I am kid?' and the kid, like I first wished would keep his mouth shut, says, 'You're flat on your ass with no gun in your hand and looking awful foolish to anyone just happening to go by, like that lady out there,' and Frisco turns to look and the kid wallops him a terrific shot on the side of the head and takes Frisco's gun out of the holster and tosses it up in the loft , and Frisco still on the floor and don't see a second of it, and no lady out there to boot, all put on by the kid, who by the way wasn't carrying a gun at the time."

"What happened then?"

"Well, it took Frisco about 10 minutes to wake hisself up and he finds no gun and looks at the kid and said, 'Where's my gun?' and the kid says, 'You go down to the saloon and wait for me and you can tell folks I was fixing it for you and if you do anything else, you ain't going to be resting easy from now on. We agree on that?' And Frisco, like his tail is you know where, nods and says okay."

Hendry recalled it all in a flash of an image and says, real loud to get the attention of everybody in the saloon, "I'm willing to tell one man how to get to McAlister on his own, that's nobody else with him, not a single other soul, but he's got to follow orders, follow my directions, do exactly as I say, or he ain't ever coming back. The one I pick has to agree to all of what I just said, don't tell anyone when he's heading out, and don't tell anybody when he gets back, if he gets back, that's just so no one can make his trail."

He kept looking at Oren Bandley who just happened to be looking back with his mouth ajar like he was about to jump on the saddle right then. Bandley said, "What does he get out of it all, the fellow you pick to go up there to Manitou's Tipi?"

"Well," smiled Hendry, "he's bound to get a chance to make some new tribes if he's onto it."

The laughter was heavy, and lots of backslapping and old fellows daring other old fellows to get up and go.

"Hey, Smitty," one old gent said to another gent across the room, "ain't you said you was ready for the Queen of Sheba she ever comes calling on you?" And they all laughed again, as loud as ever as Smitty yelled back, "That lady ain't ever met the likes of me."

And one loud voice suddenly came across the room, over the top of the laughing, like a ship's captain or a wagon master making known the orders of the day, "I'm him," Oren Bandley said, standing tall, eyes on fire, "I'm the one going up to McAlister's."

Hendry had pegged him right from the start and, as the laughter quit as quick as it had come, he said, "Seeing as you spoke up right fast, Oren, and seeing you're young enough and some good things has been said about you, I pick you to go to McAlister's, by yourself and doing all like I said here in front of all these folks who'll swear to it amen."

Smitty, enjoying the talk and laughter and the whole impossible night, said to his crony across the room, "Ain't it like I said? Mountain's the best man with the best intentions among the lot of us."

And Mountain Tooth Hendry, all his plans coming the way he designed them, capped off his evening by saying to the bartender, "Every man in the house gets a drink on me and a toast for young Oren there, outbound soon as possible on the adventure of his life."

In the early morning, birds of all kinds making noise, horses in all corrals and at the livery adding their wake-up nickers and neighs, Hendry had roused young Bandley from his sleep. "Son," he said, the sense of adventure caught up in him like the scent of a good breakfast, "it's time you got started before the town wakes up and knows what you're up to. You get yourself ready for the chance of a lifetime and I'll do whatever I can to help you out. But don't think any of this is going to be easy. You got a tough, rough road ahead of you. Mark my word well, it'll be as tough as any ever in your mind."

"What's so tough about riding up in the mountains?"

"Well, for starters, son, you ain't doing any riding except in the early part. You're plain going to walk as long as you can on this route. There's twists and there's turns and you won't make heads or tails of 'em unless you listen to me and do what I say."

"I can follow directions, but what will I be looking for? You know something about the munitions train that I ought to know? Is that all part of this?" And he relented and said, "What's all this stuff about tribe-spreading? That could be plumb interesting." He laughed as if he was only joking, but Hendry determined there was a real curiosity abounding in the young man, his eyes and spirit confirming the fact.

Hours later, they were into the heart of a canyon looking to young Bandley as if it was a dead-end canyon and no way out but back. The range of mountain peaks had loomed in front of them in the morning sunlight like tops of cone candy and both Hendry and Bandley knew they were drawn to the mountains.

"What do we do here?" Bandley said as he looked at nothing but imposing walls rising straight up around him in a near circle.

"This is where you get of your horse and go on foot, doing exactly what I tell you, which is what was told to me by McAlister hisself when I left here just like you're going to do as soon as you stop asking questions and I get through giving you proper directions you got to listen to and remember or you ain't coming back in a hurry." He sat his horse at attention, waiting for the young man to dismount.

Bandley, getting off his horse, went to pull his rifle from the scabbard and Hendry said, "Keep listening to me, son. Don't forget a word I say. I've said that enough times already to sound like an echo of myself. No rifle. No pack but what you can carry in your pockets or stuffed in your shirt. You can wear that pistol on your belt and best be it for snakes and such, and you can carry this stick here as a cane or to use as a torch when you really need it." He handed the young man a stout-looking stick.

"Do I walk around here in circles?" Bandley said as he took the stick and shook his head looking around all that appeared like prison walls rising above him.

Hendry slapped Bandley's horse on the rump and the horse ran off.

"Come down along this section, Oren, and push that stone there away from the wall. You got to skinny through there behind it, but it'll open up, high enough for you to stand" ... and paused and added ... "most times. Go the way it looks open to you. Use a torch when you have to. There's some matches in the handle. Whenever you're in doubt when the route splits, always go left like you're going away from the mountain, but you ain't. There's only one place where the route splits and you have to go right and that way is marked by my sign, which you have to find by hand. Mine and McAlister's sign both together. Mine's a plain old X and his is a T. Don't ask me what they mean, but both were easy to make in stone."

"How long'll it take me to get where I'm going, which is another question, too?"

"I got no idea how long it'll take you, Oren. I don't know how long it took McAlister either, but it took me two days and a lot of it on my belly at times."

"Tell me what I'm going to find. Don't you think I ought to know that?"

"Son, if you find it, you ain't going to leave any time in a hurry. That's a promise. And something else I got to tell you ... you won't know most times in there if it's day or night on your way in. Maybe one or two times you can see overhead if it's day because you won't really be in a tunnel, but a jumble of rocks thrown down by good old Mother Nature blocking the way and leaving a way, if you can read what she's saying in that. Old McAlister knowed it and so did I ... after a bit of deep thinking."

"You keep wrapping things up in more mystery than I ever shook my head at, Mountain" Bandley said, weighing the cudgel in his hands as if it was also to be used as a weapon.

That gesture made Hendry smile again, knowing he had picked the right man to send up in there, to McAlister's place, to Manitou's Tipi, to heaven on Earth if there really was such a place. He realized as he had a hundred other times that it was like a dream a person keeps trying to bring back but only catches pieces of it in snatches. It made him smile all over again, even the loss of something precious but faded. For a moment he thought it was like a fighter getting clobbered and knocked down and losing his senses and getting up and going right back into the action, not knowing where he'd been for a short while but sure it was elsewhere. Some things were worth the trouble.

"Ain't no fun hanging around and worrying and getting full up of questions," Bandley said, "so I guess I better get going. Keep left except one time. Use the torch for whatever. Look overhead when I can. And don't expect nothing else but something really worth all this talk." He laughed, slipped down into the hole in the canyon wall and was gone.

He heard Hendry shove the rock back in place.

Oren Bandley slipped through, squirmed, fidgeted, fought his way through openings not usually for the likes of him. He met no snakes, but heard an odd sound now and again, as though an echo was being made up in a far corner or overhead. Once, only once, he saw light above him, a thin ray of it that seemed to fall onto a smooth surface and was sent down toward him.

He measured time by what he had eaten, figuring the times his stomach seemed to cry for food, his hardtack and dried beans and jerky filling the hole in his stomach for those accountable hours between chews, but he was never sure of day or night but the one time.

Sleep had come several times along with a tiredness that grasped his whole body, and he slept off the ground on shelves of rock each time he did sleep. It was never a comfortable sleep, but did have small rewards that provided a sense of renewed energy. He had dreams in each sleep, and they seemed to focus on a group of papooses at the edge of a stream. That did set his mind on fire.

Once he got to a solid wall after a turn and went back the other way, thinking it was the right turn he had to take, but found no signs. It was much later that he thought he had taken another wrong turn, went back, lit the torch and with gnarled and bruised hands found the signs left by Hendry and McAlister. His fingers were stubby logs of aches and pains and stiffness by this time, and his legs often refused to allow him to stand upright at demand. He felt he was being bent into a new shape.

More than once he thought he was in a wild goose chase, sent off on a fool's errand by a man who was fixing up an old debt, paying off some due. No matter how many times he tried, he could find no reason why Hendry would send him on this trip out of spite or hatred or to even a score on some deed that lay forgotten in the back of his mind.

But, young, trying to recoup his energies all the time, he yet found dispiriting senses coming over him. They kept talking to him, saying what a fool he was, daring him to turn around and go back the way he had come. But that was unthinkable, probably would be worse than the way in.

In such a pother, like an object being knocked back and forth, he was squandering in a mess of possibilities, when a shaft of light came upon him, accompanied by the sound of running water, and the sense of lilacs filling the air. His spirits, suddenly in a leap, soared as he heard the soft humming voice of a woman coming from past the flash of light. Energy rammed into his legs, overcome the pains in his hands and fingers and arms from incessant crawling in tight spaces, and the stony feeling in his backbone disappeared as he heard the sweet tones of a musical voice, inhaled again the scent of lilacs as fresh as any aroma ever known in all his years.

Oren Bandley stood up without a pain in his body, his mind as clear as it would ever be, and he stepped into a swath of sunlight that came over him like a spring morning out of the grass.

A stream ran by him, the water in small twirls and currents, as it ran upon stones that formed a path across it. On the other side, washing clothes in the water, was the most beautiful girl he had ever seen, an Indian maiden no older than he was, staring at him.

She looked surprised, happy, and curious all at one time, but a smile began filling up her face like the smile had no ending.

"Ah," she said, "my father sent you. The Old One back there told me my father would send my man one day. I have waited here for six years, since I am a woman, waiting for you. My mother waits for you, for word of her husband who went to find a man for me, to come here, to walk across the bridge called Ekutsihimmiyo, connecting there and here, like heaven and earth are connected, a bridge between Shipolo and Earth."

Bandley pointed to the stones set across the stream and said, "Is that the bridge called Ekutsihimmiyo, connecting here and there. Like heaven and earth can be connected, a bridge between Shipolo and Earth?"

"No," the beautiful maiden said, "that is it there, where you have just walked. That is Ekutsihimmiyo. You have made the journey. I am here for you. For six years I have been waiting for you. The Great Spirit has sung his song for me at last. I am White Bird of the Lilac, and you will be my man this very day. And my mother, Mountain Dove, and my father, wherever he is, will rejoice."

White Bird took the hand of Oren Bandley and led him across the stones, after he had tossed aside the cudgel and his gun belt, as she suggested. "There is no need here, in Manitou's Tipi, for such things."

She pointed to a place behind him and another cudgel and another gun belt lay on the ground. "Those are my father's," she said. "They will be here forever, as will yours."

White Bird of the Lilac placed her cheek on the shoulder of Oren Bandley. "From this very moment, I am your woman. I am your woman forever and ever. It is like my mother belongs to my father for ever and ever. They are one as we will be one no matter where we are in this life. It is just like the Great Spirit Manitou told me, I have been one man's woman since the day I was born and I have waited all this time for you. Now, come with me and see where my father was years ago, here," and she pointed over a mall rise into a most beautiful valley snug in the mountains.

"In Manitou's Tipi, my home forever and ever. Is it not beautiful?" She gestured again, a sweeping gesture that encompassed wonders that hit Bandley like a ton of stone.

He saw grazing animals, lodges and teepees of all kinds and colors, Indians in full dress, maidens in colors from the keenest rainbow, warriors in pelts and skins and blue coats of a faded hue he knew were army residue. It seemed a hundred children played in the sunlight, or fished at the stream or watered and fed animals or sat on a pile of logs telling stories to younger children. Couples walked hand in hand, at times trailed by little ones.

"My people, with the help of Manitou and McAlister, who were brothers by the blooded knife, saved over a thousand lives when they stole the whole shipment from a huge army ammunition train and Indian braves and soldiers brought it in here piece by piece. It took them a whole year, but none of it was ever used. Imagine that, a thousand lives on both sides, and some of the soldiers are here yet, raising their families, not going back to the horrors of war, to death and destruction. Manitou says we will live here forever in peace. Peace lives here in our midst. Peace fills us. Peace stays in place. Are you not pleased, my man? White Dove of the Lilac is pleased that her man has come across Ekutsihimmiyo to me, to us, to meet my mother, to sit at the fire tonight with Manitou while the stars shine down on us like you have never seen stars, even out on your grass on sleepless nights. They shine their peace here on us, bringing messages from the Great Spirit, saying journeys begin and end but we must make the choosing on our own. You have made a journey to me."

Awed by all he saw, Bandley said, "Is this McAlister's? Did I really get to McAlister's?"

Twenty years later, long after Ship Mountain Tooth Hendry had died in a buffalo stampede, and his remains brought to Munitions Mount for proper burial, and numberless stories went on being told in The Chauncy Remney Saloon and House of Good Taste and Better Scents, about his being '"lost up in them mountains for a spell," a middle aged rancher came into town for a visit. He was a vibrant looking blond-headed man, had a distinction about him that said "he had been places," and the assessment was not charitable but was an honest one. And he looked familiar to some patrons who stared at him for long moments.

The visitor walked to the bar and ordered a shot and a beer. He told the bartender he was from Tobacco Shelf, which was north a ways in the same mountain range, and he admitted, after questioning, that he had a ranch and a stable of horses back there at Tobacco Shelf that were the envy of many riders in the region.

The visitor chuckled as he told the story and his familiarity grew on a few of the customers in The Chauncy Remney Saloon and House of Good Taste and Better Scents. One of the patrons said, at the same time the bartender said it, "Hey, ain't you Oren Bandley who was lost up in them mountains just like Mountain Tooth was?"

Every person in the saloon at that moment knew the story about Mountain Tooth Hendry and the kid he sent off on his own adventure, Oren Bandley, gone from the area around Munitions Mount for years upon years, feared dead in the mountains, out of sight and out of mind.

From the far side of the room, off in a corner as if he had been forgotten, an older gent said, "You goin' to tell us anythin' new?" Sumpthin' we ain't heard yet. I get plain tired of old folks and old tales. What's new, sonny boy?" He slapped his thighs like he was a dancer doing tricks on stage.

The rustling and shuffling began in earnest around the room, curiosity coming up in a hurry as though it had been buried too long in The Chauncy Remney Saloon and House of Good Taste and Better Scents.

The barkeep, evidently a good business man, set up another beer and shot for the visitor now identified as Oren Bandley, lost man like Mountain Tooth was, a pure legend standing right there in front of him, in his bar. It was money rolling into the till.

Bandley, raising his glass, said, "Any whelps here ain't married and want to tell me about themselves? I'm sure interested."

In the back of the room, near the door where light shone on his blond head, a young man stood up.

Jehrico and the Cock-Eyed Burro

The townspeople of Bola City began laughing at Jehrico Taxico and his new cock-eyed burro just as he started into the town. He was returning to town from a junkie's jaunt and haunt as he might have called it. He heard the snickers, the titters, the sneaky laughter coming from, of all places, the slopped pen where pigs dug their ways through the day, then at the livery where a few poor folk of town labored for endless hours for measly nickels. Then at the side of Grunty's blacksmith shop where a midget Mexican carried coal and wood to keep the fire hot and managed, every now and then, to almost set the place on fire. For a nickel a day, Bib Grunty could put up with a fire possibly bigger than what he wanted. He didn't believe in insurance, which was a word he did not know.

The story of the burro ran ahead of Jehrico right to the heart of Bola City, from the initial encounter of a freighter and Jehrico way out on the town road.

Lagon Brick started it at Hagen's Saloon just as the beer spigot was opened for the first drink. "D'ja hear what Jehrico come up with this time? He's got himself a cock-eyed burro who can't see one way and the other way is blind as a bat." He laughed so hard the few customers got caught up in the news. "So dumb he is he don't know when a rock's put in the sack on his back. It's what Doc Fenton says is 'a dumb animal working the back end of forever.' Don't that say it better than none of us can say it ... 'the back end of forever.'" He leaned over the bar and laughed so hard he almost threw up his beer, but managed to hold on to it. He too knew the nickel side.

The barkeep, in a loud, tenor's voice, said, "Where'd he get a cock-eyed burro, Lag?"

"Some injun beat him at the junk game. Swapped him straight up for Jehrico's gun, 'cause I swear he knew Mildred was dead no more'n a week from that hunk of wire she ate straight out. He knew Jehrico was in the straits, and pressed for all he's worth."

He shook his head in disbelief. "'Magine losing an old maid like Mildred 'cause she ate a hunk of wire, and getting' a cock-eyed substitute? Life ain't no fun unless you look it straight in the eye." He ended up again over the bar and said, "You can't ask no cock-eyed burro to do that for you, can you?"

At that most appropriate moment, Jehrico Taxico walked into Hagen's Saloon.

His burro was with him, with big ears and the ugly eye.

The bad eye was indeed an ugly, engorged yellow-green thing that looked as if it had exploded within itself. One of the early ladies, standing at the foot of the stairs that lead to the rooms above, nearly fainted at the sight of the swollen green-yellow eye.

Hysteria ensued to a certain level until Jehrico raised his hand and said, "Look what my burro found for me." And he held up a sparkling diamond that looked as bright as the evening star. It indeed shone like the evening star all by itself in the western sky. It mesmerized a few of the men and all of the ladies, the shine so brilliant coming through the rough edges of a ruffian of the fold, a found beauty.

"Ain't that somethin',?" Jehrico said, as he wiped the stone on his shirt. "Right there in front of me it was and I didn't catch one glitter of it. Bessie here," and with that he patted the burro on the head, "she just kicked her foot into the ground and up it popped, as perty as a trout in the stream lookin' for that special worm a mine."

The barkeep said, "Let me look at that stone, Jehrico, see if I can tell what you might get if you was to sell it."

The silence came into the room like shadows move; no voices, no edges, no substance, just the eerie expectation of riches beyond dreams for one of them, for the junk collector, Jehrico Taxico and his cock-eyed burro he called Bessie.

The barkeep studied the stone for a long while, messages moving back and forth across his face like as though he was a signalman on the railroad. "Looks like the best I've ever seen, Jehrico. That's a real piece, man. I'd go hide it now case someone was thinkin' of stealin' it." He flashed his eyes in disbelief of the find and its value.

"No problem there, Nate," Jehrico said. "I believe Bessie got her eye on a whole field of them things, and it's the bad eye to boot." His laughter was joined by all in the room. "Ain't that somethin' for a half blind fool to find herself so rich she don't care who knows it."

From the back of the room a voice yelled out, "Where was you, Jehrico, when Bessie did her kickin'? You anywhere near that old Fuller mine that was diggin' for gold and found nothin'? Wouldn't that beat all?"

"How'd you know that, Jigger? You bin out there recently explorin' around?"

"Nah," said Jigger as he withdrew into his corner.

Jehrico took a carrot from his pocket and fed it to Bessie, letting her take a nibble at a time, her teeth like wide boards in a painted fence, the chewing as loud as pigs in a sty.

"Ole Bessie was right on goin' by when she changed her mind for somethin' or other, and it was dang good she done that. That there stone lit up like a lamp in the middle of the night, all flarin' and beautiful like it was talkin' to me. This is money, it was sayin', lots of money. I coulda choked on my goodness at that minute, choked myself to death. Easy as sayin' it, it was."

At the far end of the room, three men had already slipped out a side door and the hoof beats came back into the room like drum beats from a tattoo on a far hilltop.

Another fellow in the back of the room said, "You know where they're aheadin', don't you, Jehrico? They's lookin' for a head start on diamond findin', don't you know?"

"Oh, them fellas is goin' in the wrong direction. I didn't mean the Fuller place out on the Bola City road toward Lattimer, but the Fuller place where they's been buried all these years, and that ain't nowhere near Boot Hill either, as most all of you know, 'cept I suppose them fellas on the run now."

The barkeep winked at Jehrico Taxico and the whole place lit up as he rolled an apple down the bar for Bessie, Jehrico Taxico's new cock-eyed burro and salter of diamond fields.

Jehrico's Sign

It was Collie Sizemore, Jehrico's pal from day one, himself a Bola City person of interest, who was on the soap box in Hagen's Saloon, Marshy Headland keeping tabs on him for his boss, "Collie knowing a little about everything," as some customers often said, "and everything about a little," as Headland's boss might say, and did say. That hidden boss of Headland's was afoot with a new plan for making more money and Jehrico was in the way, harmless as he always appeared, the Midas from Mexico, the Merlin from Mexico, the Make-do-with-anything from Mexico, the wetback who was high and dry from the very beginning of his first hunt for throw-offs and cast-offs and trailside junk. It was Collie who said right up front, "He's Bola City's Best Collector of Bountiful Crap. BC, in other words, and having nothing whatever to do with Time when the Good Lord appeared on Earth or the college starting to jump around back there in the city of Boston, starting about 1864 in large bounds.

"That damned Magician from Mexico," Headland's boss had cursed aloud, "has an eye for infinity and eternity and an ear for celestial musical chimes of brass and cast iron bells born with tunes built right into their coming, shapes of them, true shapes, not yet realized." A profound thief, he was, at his profound best, knowing that Collie knew that Jehrico had a jumping start ahead of the head man in the area .... for now.

"By gosh," Jehrico was thinking, "it sure is good having Collie around. He's worth more than the day will be worth," and at that moment he could realize the potential of the junk he had gathered the day before from a fire site, his old mule Mildred piled up, backside and two-wheeled trailer of sorts loaded to the brim with "found stuff."

Collie, if he heard that spiel of Headland's boss, could never accept second place behind it. As Collie spouted again for all to hear, and especially Jehrico, he had his eye on Jehrico and his mind on Headland, aware of the connections, "the stuff in the background that grounds on your back," so ably put that only Jehrico picked it up, and then Collie got to the gist of the matter.

"Jehrico, you have to advertise, advertise, advertise. I've been saying that in triplicates by the numbers all the way up to the 9th dance on the card." He put his hands on his hip (his way of announcing a coming announcement) and said, "What's your sign, Jehrico? Where is it? I Ain't seen nary a smidgeon's pigeon of it. It's advertising any way possible, every way possible. Put up a sign. Put up a dozen signs. A hundred of them. Let everybody know you're around and have a sweet deal for them. I'd be your manager but I've got other obligations at the moment."

The congregation's titter was a congregation's guffaw, loud as possible in the tightly packed room. Where Jehrico drew customers for his junk, at a good profit you can imagine, Collie drew a crowd for his reviews, his stage plays, his dramas of the west. "He's about as good as we'll ever get around here," one customer might say to another one at the bar or a table where elbows kicked off messages, a body language reader's sense of the natural moves of a natural man in his milieu.

Jehrico, at the moment, just nodded at Collie's trying to incite additional actions on his part, making the day interesting, grabbing hold on what Jehrico might say in his born language, tempered a bit by his loss of family, early freedom on the trails and the wide prairies, and his successive and moveable adoptions for one cause or another, which we know Collie called out like a repeating rifle at work, "his higher enrollments in the school of knocks."

Collie, gifted in so many ways, which Jehrico also found "when he turned him over for inspection that long-ago day of first introduction," said in Spanish, *'No habrá paro este huérfano Mexicano y empresario una vez que llegue algo de publicidad en las paredes del mundo occidental . Un día se va a limpiar los callejones de Chicago , Boston y Nueva York , ya que se puso en su camino.'* " And some of the audience in the saloon, with enough times across the border, of course, or having employed good *vaqueros* as trail hands, explained to others what they heard as, "There'll be no stopping this Mexicano orphan and entrepreneur once he gets some advertising on the walls of the western world. One day he'll clean the back alleys of Chicago, Boston and New York because they got in his way."

Jehrico, due home to Lupalazo's lap and kitchen, merely said, "How many signs would please your idea of a great advertising campaign, Collie?" The idea ticked him. It sounded good for business.

Ahead of the game, whip-smart and whip-started, his blue eyes flashing quick significance, energy never lacking on his brow, at attention's command, Collie said, without a smile, "Jehrico's always in the mix, when it comes to pick-up sticks, hang a thousand signs on roadside trails, he'll take your junk in awesome bails, make junk do for all of you." He slapped his hand down on the bar and the barkeep, long a fan of both Collie and Jehrico, popped another free drink on the bar. "You keep this up today, Collie, and I might get you drunk as sin."

In the round of laughter following, all patrons favoring any bartender's attempt at humor, good or bad, drinks tempered in such likenesses, roared their approval as Jehrico slipped easily and unseen from the saloon, even Collie missing his departure, the soapbox still his "milieu in the middle," which often passed his lips.

Shortly later, in her creative warmth, incurably beautiful both in face and figure, holding their youngest child to her full breast, Lupalazo kissed Jehrico without missing one sweep in the mixing bowl. "You look pleased, Mister Junkie. Have you found gold or jewels, or did a visit to Hagen's strike you with other goodness?" She didn't wait for an answer, and didn't hesitate one bit in kissing him again, crossed her face with a sign of thought, and said, "Was Collie there? What's he have to say today? Any gems galore?" She giggled thinking how she could talk like Collie, smiled, comforted the baby now owning the name Ox-ford, and added, "You look like Collie swallowed the mouse or the puma. He have you on another escapade or exploration? Is that so? Have I hit it rightly?" Slightly, deliberately, she shifted into a stance that Jehrico highly favored and brought with him on trailside adventure. It was enough to keep her man company in the wilds.

He marveled again at woman's intuition, the spare parts they carried for motivation, self-preservation, secrets no man held, their hands and minds directly on fate, destiny and the matters of life at the moment. Collie was right on the nail head when he first assessed Jehrico's new woman, there being no "old woman" for him, no "other woman."

"What discarded, cast-off books of greatness have you been reading lately, Sweetest Trade I ever made?" He saw her again, proud, defiant, astride the Indian pony at the juncture of their lives, the beginning.

"Well, Mr. Taxico, I have had a delicious time with some of your box of Beadle's *New Dime Novels,* the ones with colored covers you pulled out of the dance hall that burned in Riverton. I can still smell the smoke in the pages, as though it was gunfire atop its last reading. The writers there know the language quite well." She laughed at his puckish surprise and kissed him again, at which move he found new son Ox-ford in his arms.

"How is that for a trade?" she said, and followed it up by almost qualifying her widest smile. "Have you forgotten already that today, this date, is the one we settled on for your birthday. The children are excited beyond reason for the picky day." The trace of irony was humorous, suited her smile, the warmth of her kitchen; he smelled the celebration pies. Of necessity, there was more than one pie.

Sometime near the beginning of the year, Jehrico established the most likely date of his birth on a trip to Mexico, when an old man in a small mountain side village, said, "You look like the man who used to live in that house down there," pointing out a small adobe house at the end of the village. "You're the spitting image of him. He died fighting a desperate band of men and his wife died many years ago from a sickness because their son was taken off by another family and no one never saw him again. If you are that boy, you were born on the morning of the 29th day in the month of March and that makes you an Aries wearing the horns of the ram."

Jehrico was thunderstruck, but the old man continued with his strange tale: "I don't know if you looked like the mother's family, but you are a long look in still water at her husband's face, at the face I have no doubt belonged to your father. My old problem is that I have no memory of names. None at all. Faces? Yes. Names? Nothing. Sometimes I forget my mother's name before she came to my father as a near child, as they told me, from the heart of the mountains, weeping for a place to put down her head, hungry as a deserted cub. They said she slept a whole year beside my father before she became a woman and my mother, and he was a shepherd's boy who became a man."

The old man had told the story partly in his own tongue and partly in English. But a curiosity flourished on his face and with a slow turn he moved completely into the old language and told the same story in the most comfortable words: *"No sé si parecía que la familia de la madre, pero es un largo vistazo en agua a su marido, en la cara no me cabe duda pertenecía a su padre. Mi viejo problema es que no tengo memoria de los nombres. Ninguno en absoluto. Rostros? Sí. Nombres? Nada. A veces me olvido mi nombre de la madre antes de que ella vino a mi padre como un niño, como me dijeron, en el corazón de las montañas, el llanto de un lugar para poner su cabeza, hambriento como un cachorro abandonado. Nos dijeron que se durmió un año entero al lado de mi padre antes de que ella se convirtió en una mujer, y mi madre, y que él era un pastor joven que se convirtió en un hombre."*

Jehrico, knowing the old man was turning himself inside out for him, understood the man's loss and his own gain. The keen memory of one man had slipped down the side of a mountain and another man had found in the deep ravine a birthday to celebrate with his own family. It was another discovery for one man given over to junk collection, and he knew this one was pure silver all the way.

Jehrico carried the tale with him until Lupalazo, with children beginning to clamor for birthday celebrations, broke it loose. The celebrations would start on the next time March 29th that came upon them.

And as Taxico family history has it, still working its way into odd pages in odd places, it fell in line with Collie's suggestion or demand for an advertisement effort by Jehrico for his work.

The Mexican Wizard of sorts, thinking about Collie's stance, his innumerable hints at growth of Jehrico's investments, faced a takeover of his assets, now most considerable. There might be a gaining of ground by Marshy Headland's boss, a spark beginning at first light.

Jehrico considered all things, including Collie Sizemore's friendship, intuition, intelligence. At one point of ideas, at a surge of one of them, he summoned his eldest son and gave him instructions.

It was a simple design and said in English, "**Jehrico's Sign**" accompanied by the ♈ ARIES symbol, the horns of a ram.

There were a dozen such signs attached to various structures in and around Bola City.

Collie Sizemore, genius at get-up and go-fer, unrestrained melodies and poetical dramas and comedies galore, at short cuts in the art of language, who loved *Abbreviations Galore* (his distinctive claim being the reduction in identification of things, as if he wanted to be spared of too much speech), upstaged by the Mexican junkie, was the lone man in all of Bola City who laughed himself drunk that night in Hagen's Saloon.

Chase Holman's Kidnapping
(or Mountain Man and Miniatures)

I have little to say on the matter of young Chase Holman's kidnapping, but what follows closely here is sworn as the truth from my humble soul and eyes that rarely want for targets. I'm a hunter, a mountain man, was born to ride, live and die in whatever hills or mountains I loved, and know lead only in the form of bullets. I never knew the first thing about lead soldiers or other toy warriors such as Indians and cowboys. I'm just plain old me, Edward Joseph Dundeen, mostly known as Edjo, a Highlander by birth, an American by disturbed allegiance and displacement and an adventurer on the move. In the dark I'd tell a lady I'm six feet of muscle, sport a red beard thick as a rug, and have few limitations, if any, with weapons; in bright dawn I'd listen to their proposals.

Down from the mountains I had come, my horse Scallywag a mite skittish, his ears better than mine, telling me to stay alert, my two mules packed up with four months catch of furs of all kinds and magnitudes, and a big hole in all my appetites. I was headed for Juice Slattery's place in New Holman, first. Juice'd buy a bucket of old grease from me; I had a good eye, a steady hand and once saved him from an unfair altercation with three bullets for two men bound to run off with his wagon and goods. He even offered to buy their horses, from me, at a fair price, "Mine for the takin'," as they say out here.

New Holman, I'll have you know, sits on the prettiest shelf on the Humboldt River, where enough dreams brought it into place and a whole bunch of greed later on knocked it into the next century on its hands and knees. But all that's beyond my reach.

This day, the day of the kidnapping of Chase Holman's and wife Grace's only son, was a cool September day, a damned good day for selling all my furs to Juice, and I was bound for town when I saw two riders heading for the hills, and one of them had a blanket slung across the saddle with him. It didn't look like it was empty, and then I saw a pair of boots dangling out from the end of the blanket. They could belong to a pal shortly dead and bound for burial way up on some lonely hill, but I doubted it ... twice I saw the boots kick, meaning pain, discomfort or downright displeasure.

When the two riders swung up into the Saucer Canyon, at a steady trot, they did not see me ... and I kept out of sight until they were out of sight.

I thought about it for a while, going in up there, taking a peek at them, but I had the furs to take care of ... which meant winter's grub and drink and ammo. If I didn't have that stuff, Juice'd have to take me in, stash me up in his hay mow and, when and if he had a winter drunk on, he'd forget what I had done for him. I'd spent one winter with him, up in his mow; I'd freeze before I'd do it again.

Anyway, once they were out of sight, and my wandering mind came back under my hat, I turned for town, the long haul working on me. The place is named for Chase Holman, cowman, rancher, builder, owner of much, but smart as a whistle on a windy day. He named it because he built it and wanted it this way. He owned most of it, as I said, but let others in to get some of the spoils ... and take some of the headaches, like the general store and one of the two saloons and the hotel above the general store and the funeral parlor attached to the livery and the store for ladies only ... but he owned, lock, stock and wagons, the freight hauling rights from and to Elko and any place in between. If you wanted to stock your shelves, stock your bar, put goods in your store window, Chase Holman brought it in or shipped it out as sold.

When I got to Holman, the place was in a turmoil, noise galore, women crying on the street, drunks at sudden and honest sobering, and Juice yelling at me first thing he saw me, "You see anythin' out there on the trail, Ace? Anythin' funny? Holman's kid's been kidnapped. That boy's a special kid, a genius, makes them little lead figures I told you about and showed you couple of 'em; the cowpokes and Injuns and the soldiers, too, from Shiloh and Gettysburg and them other battles of the Big War. Chase is gonna kill somebody over this. And to throw the rope on it all, Grace collapsed right there in the middle of the street. Some kid handed her a note that a cowpoke gave him a dollar to deliver by hand. She read it, screamed, and collapsed in the middle of the street, in all that dirt and dust, with her best duds on, that yellow dress we all liked her in and them big yellow you-know-whats prouder'n any mountains we ever knowed."

You have to know I'm not the smartest thing ain't been to school yet, but I said nothing about what I'd seen. There'd be more coming, and I'd let Chase Holman handle that. Hell, he just about handled everything else in town, and as far as Saucer Canyon, too, I figured, with only me in the way, in line with what had already sort of filtered into my mind, things with me working as slow as walking to church.

At first, I'd only seen a couple of the kid's lead soldiers, one a Blue and one a Gray and one cowpoke all painted up like he just jumped up to face a fast draw in town, hand up, gun out, him leaning towards the other shooter. Even his Stetson sat on his back, the drawstring like it was holding it in place. It was all so damned real it give me the chills on my backside. Kid does it good, making them things. 'Course, it was Juice who showed me first, that little piece of a shooter, because little Chase has Phil Sligo, the blacksmith, make up them iron molds he pours the melted lead into and makes the figures right quick. Kid draws pictures and Phil goes to work ... between horseshoeing and wheel rims and such ... like he's living in the kid's mind. Young Chase came up with the idea all himself when his father brought a couple of figures back from Chicago one time, soldiers from Europe, like knights of King Arthur or some king. Makes Chase say his kid ain't ever going to be a cowman but play with toy soldiers his whole life, but admits he started it all hisself."

Then, on an errand, I'd seen the ranks of his lead figures, all kinds of them, as he had scattered them in scenic battle sites in a section of the ranch yard between the bunkhouse and the barn ... and woe to any ranch hand who disturbed any of the battle scenes the way young Chase had set them up, all from hearing stories and reading the books his father had shipped in from Chicago. Besides all that, some lucky veterans of our big war on both sides, said, "The kid's got it pretty well lined up, the way it was on July 1, 1863, Seminary Ridge, Gettysburg, Pennsylvania, and that meant the possible location of General Lee's Headquarters."

And those wily and lucky veterans said the same about Second Manassas, and General Longstreet's Assault, August 30, 1862. And he had squared away about 7 or 8 other famous sites from around the world, right out of books, history's pages, mind you, the Knights and the Yeomen and the awful arrow brigades ... and it was like a history lesson sitting there on a bench built against the barn and listening to the little shaver knock the hell out of losing generals for their faulty plans and lack of battle visions.

But back to the kid otherwise, and his plight: It was Grace who got it all going, though ... the posse, a deputy who went around and questioned everybody in town about anything they might have seen or freighters, wagon haulers, and coachmen, calling all the ladies (outside of the saloon ones) into the church to pray in one bunch, even as snobby as some can get. Now I like Gracie, I like to tell you, but I don't have much use for her husband, especially when he's plotting on more green in the till anyways it comes, meaning he don't care for them or me.

And it was Gracie who let out the word in church that her husband was going to offer $1000 for the safe return of his son, and $2000 for the kidnappers dead or alive. Shows what kind of man he was, or father, or husband, or citizen for that matter ... vengeance thicker than love or blood. But she knew the reward information would drag men from their sick beds if need be, or from the arms of their mistresses or from another man's payroll even if his job wasn't done. Nobody saw much of $1000 or $2000 those days but Chase Holman, then the banker, or the next bank robber ... and that might be coming up on the list of things to do tomorrow for some folks thereabouts, including those two riders I spotted dipping into Saucer Canyon.

Juice, glad to see me otherwise, and having a shot ready for me soon as he saw me coming into town loaded down with furs and trying to mellow me for a lower price, said, as if hailing a fountain of information, "Edjo, the boys tell me those two hombres with young Chase headed out to the north from the ranch, like they was headed in your direction, right along the rim to Saucer Canyon and a hundred places to hide up in the other end with all the narrow lead-offs and skinny tunnels and passageways. They don't have to have a secret cabin to hide out; they's enough holes in there to hide a herd of cows, you had a mind and the time." He rubbed his hands together the same way a jeweler does for a prospective groom or a just-married husband coming off a long drive.

I had ideas and visions of the far end of the canyon, a maze if there ever was one, hundreds of caves and deep shelves and crevices with no end and peep holes by the thousand to keep an eye on trailers and stalkers and posses galore. Juice told me about Handsome Henry Hoss, shooter, killer, bank robber, known by the only name he ever had, even the one on his wanted poster in a dozen areas of the country and him up in there for three months without sight or sound of him. "That Injun," Juice related for a second time in the evening, "Two Feathers, slim as a weasel crawlin', smelled him out one night from Hoss's late supper fire in the rock hole he stashed himself in. Laid a rawhide noose in the dark, spread some bear blood on the rope that Hoss would smell, and caught him by both ankles and yanked him upright and got the reward for Hoss."

"Three months?" I said.

"Yup, and never a sight or a sound. His horse had been shot and cut up, but that meat wouldn't last more than a week or so even if he smoked it for the whole week. For sure, other things live in there in the rocks, or under them, and all of 'em hungry as Satan."

The thing about Juice is he's smarter than most of the others, and of course smarter than me, yet I figured he knew all along that I was about to go up into Saucer Canyon after the $1000 or the $2000 or all of it in one roping and was already working my mind over what lay up in there, the way he explained all of it again, how it might look to a man hiding or looking, take your pick.

I was out there where I last saw them, the pair of kidnappers as they headed into Saucer Canyon.

Overhead, at a discrete angle nearer evening than morning, sun rays golden as corn and beginning the first of angular landings, a coyote calling as if on my tail, when I saw the glint of light, a reflection lasting a bare second, in the grass of a worn path, enough light to catch my eye and my interest. You had to hand it to that Holman kid ... it was one of his lead soldiers; this one a yeoman with bow and quiver and kneeling on one knee as though he had sighted his prey ... as I figured I had a solid lead too.

I imagined him, as he was being grabbed, stuffing his shirt with some of his true loves living in constant lead. Did he have enough to lead the whole way to a hideaway? Was he forced to guess and measure them out, one at a time, a trail turn at a time? Did he know the territory? I thought he was about the smartest kid I had met in all my days; and just hoped he had a sense of timing and direction, and the evil intentions of his abductors, to put me right where they were tucked away in the canyon. The kid had a way with him, that's for sure.

The second poured-lead lead, unpainted, sparkled where the trail turned to the left; not an abrupt turn, but enough so that I assumed he could feel or see somehow that a change had come to the course the two horses of the kidnappers were on. I didn't know if he was able to peek outside the blanket he was rolled in, knew the terrain from limited sight or a familiarity with the whistle of winds through tunnels and crevices. They carried known gusto and echoes, notes that old prospectors could recognize in a jiffy; not like the notes on a saloon piano shared with women, whiskey and noise, but the way windy rocks can bring a song to a real songsmith, the tune coming off sheer and thin edges, no less than from the strings on a west-trekking wagoner's violin, a midnight banjo upgrading a campfire, or a man with a secretly-held affinity for a song and a sweet voice.

This next discovered miniature critter was an amputated cowboy, some accident within the mold, or close after it was retrieved from the iron grip, being the cause of a missing leg. Why hadn't the kid tossed him away, or back into the melting pot? But he looked like a good old boy, a drover, a horse-breaker, not a gambling townie, but a cowpoke just cut short on prime activities ... no more dances, no partner, no chasing the girls, stuck in place with his tongue hanging out for the rest of his life. A ream of fictional sadness thumped me with its honesty, the kind that blazes at the back of your head at surprise revelations. The truth of that kind of stuff gets to me, I swear on my sleeve.

Still, I wondered what was next for young Chase; if he was running out of lead. I swear, that made me quickly check my guns, even as a hint of laughter slipped out of me ironic as hell, my horse Scallywag shaking his head in attention or appreciation of circumstances. I was in with a pretty good set of friends, Scallywag and a kid who without a doubt knew his way around most things, and me hoping Saucer Canyon was one of them, me wondering again how he got along with his father, if the clutching, money-hungry gent ever rode up here with his son, sort of a Father-Son outing on horseback; I doubted it, but hoped it was possible - at least once anyway.

Ahead of me, the trail bent a number of ways through masses of fallen rocks, sheered slabs that hundreds of years earlier had slid down the face of the mountain to stand erect in earth, like slabs of pie off a tin oven plate. Scallywag, on his own, was slowed down and picking his way through rugged terrain on the canyon floor where the sun seemed to have collected a sudden ball of heat. It made me check my canteen to make sure it was filled. Long ago juice had advised me, "Water and your horse are more important than any girl you'll ever meet."

I used to laugh at Juice. But the advice seemed factual now, foretold, as the heat magnified in places, only to drop away again, and that made my mind switch to tunnels and crevices and caves without ends. I wished for a map that could expose all the secret places where the kidnappers were holed up. They had to be here, I argued with myself, because sooner or later they'd have to get in touch with Chase the elder, get into town in the darkness, hide their intentions, get their demands across to the paymaster, and get back out of town to hide and not have to ride 100 miles to do all that ... and keep a bright kid tight in place. I could imagine him being a handful to his captors.

The hoof beats of Scallywag echoed as we moved along, sounding as loud as alarm signals. If they were listening, my prey, they'd hear me; if they were too deeply hidden in a rocky chamber, they might not hear the near-rhythmic hoof beats. The whole musical presentation of Saucer Canyon was both mysterious and commonly usual for windy, rocky places, though I hoped that such salient expositions might somehow be curbed under the conditions of search.

Such an appreciation for the landscape stressed around me, made one helluva target for any shooter hiding behind a big rock slab, prone in a dark cave with his rifle trained on me tall in the saddle.

I swept myself off the saddle and alit nimbly, ducking at the same time behind Scallywag, hiding the target of my heart, my gun hand, dead center in my Stetson holding the sun off my gaze.

Stopping now and then seemed wise, and I progressed in meager steps, listening, harkening to windy sounds the way they moved, emanating from a thunderous collection of stony paths, cliff walls, hidden ways more secret than ant trails once under cover of earth. And I thought more often of the $1000 reward for getting young Chase back home to his mom's kitchen than I did about the $2000 for getting the scoundrels that had drawn me out here, sooner or later to get shot at than I figured earlier.

It was at that precise moment that I saw, not one, but two lead-cast toy wranglers, unpainted as yet in ranch colors and but feet apart, without the distances between them like the others I'd found. Chase had dropped them to alert a posse, perhaps his father, or some head-strong idiot like me, hell-bent on heroics and money-grabbing for the moment. Instantly, I tucked Scallywag behind a 12-foot slab standing about eight feet away from the cliff face, patted him with love and tenderness, let him lick my hand, muttered, "Good old boy, you hide awhile in the shade. Good old Scallywag."

Something told me, young Chase told me, in the unspoken words of these tiny critters, strangers becoming my friends, that I was pretty close to where I wanted to go. Big hints, big clues, from the little ones of his own, somewhat private world; the world of discarded lead, old inker's lead dumped for some reason, clumps of lead from odd fire-sights, lead from a long standing target range might have stood behind his pa's barn longer than his toy-favoring son had lived; the kid had brought it all to one destiny of little critters of his own choice. And they were working for me now, my posse of sorts. I had to hold back another small titter of irony.

I left my rifle in the sheath of my saddle, took pistol to hand, and saw the crevice where I could have brought my horse ... and where their horses might have been led, Chase aboard lighter than he started, with them. It opened, the crevice, not directly to me as I faced it, but at an angle, appearing much slimmer than it was, like an illusion of sorts, a game of shadows and light engaged for surprise. With the sudden appearance of the slot in the wall, I slipped my spurs quickly from my boots and tucked them in the saddle bag. This close, I thought, and Chase telling me so by the close placement of the last two lead toys, that they had directed me to the hidden entrance, like scouts out ahead of the patrol ... and that this pair of them would be the last such alerts ... that he had no more lead miniatures to track his trail.

I moved slowly, quietly, edging my way on, my hands always on a wall, keeping low, trying not to be a target. Time dragged along with me. I wondered how the kidnappers were treating the kid, wondered if they knew who they really had in tow; probably not what they thought in the beginning.

Suddenly, I was into the heart of the mountain it seemed, as it broadened out and up, yet continued to be, even in singular presentations, a huge, formidable labyrinth, most definitely a place not to get lost in, get separated from your senses. I was surprised, and pleased, to smell smoke, burnt food smoke, beef, pork and bread. Coffee was on, too. The sense of smell, at least, was working well. Then, I heard voices, undecipherable at first, mumbling mostly, words being cut up by jagged rocks, sharp turns, and with a further few steps into the apparent opening of another room of the mountain, I heard a strange voice say, "What do you do with it then, kid?"

Oh, boy, it sounded like the kidnapped kid had the kidnappers in tow.

"Oh," came the voice of Chase Holman, Jr., young and spritely and carrying no fear, but full of honest interest, "then when the whole pot is melted, I pour a certain amount, not too much of it, into as many of the molds as I can. You know, those are the molds Mr. Sligo the blacksmith made for me just the way I drew them for him."

Another voice said, "He already told you that stuff, Cage. Didn't you hear him? The kid's too sharp for you. You gotta watch your step or he'll dump the whole damned thing right on top of us. We'll be stuck in a cave without a paddle."

"Oh, shut up, Scotia, that ain't so funny. You're always worried about something going wrong. Any little thing throws you right off the saddle. Be loose, man, he's only a kid, but I wish I knew what he knows when I was a kid. Just look at this. Why this one's the perfect little drover of the herd. Everything about him is perfect. Look at that, will ya!"

I could imagine the sight, Chase already owning one of them, and using the last miniature toy cowboy as his last argument, his final deal, throwing the other one into befuddlement, worry, capture, the rewarding end of the line. He'd be in his Mom's kitchen in a matter of hours, having three-minute eggs or a day-long soup off the back end of her stove, sure as shooting.

It all went through me in a hurry. I saw all the pictures, all the images, all the ideas taking shape, saw young Chase hug his Mom, saw his father hand over the reward money and hating to do so, a grimace accompanying each and every note of currency passed over to me. I managed to entertain myself with a thought, "That's a lot of frown for one man," and the giggle was honest.

I thought it all over; handling the two of them, once captured, would be tough getting them into town. I had to wing one of them, keep him out of it, and just worry about the other one. Chase had to know where their horses were; I couldn't lug them out or walk them out, not out of Saucer Canyon.

One shot and it had to be good, had to be a surprise, had to make sure Chase was out of the way.

It was perfect ... when I stepped slowly out and into view, my pistol aimed at them, their backs to me, Chase seeing me first, dropped the last lead wrangler at his feet, went to his knees to retrieve it, and I shot the right hand of one of them: I didn't know which one. But my aim was immediately on the other.

I wagged the gun for a slight move. "Drop your gun belt or you're dead right there where you stand."

The wounded one, Scotia by name by his voice now screaming with pain, made a left-handed drop of his gun belt. It fell to the rocky floor with a solid sound. Chase grabbed it and ran to one side. The kid was quick, I thought, in admiration. He'd be ready for grow-up time before it came down the road to him.

The other kidnapper, now known to me as Cage, and to the whole town soon enough, and to the paymaster, dropped his belt too, pistol still in place in the holster. Chase scurried and got that one too.

"Chase" I said, "my name's Edjo Dundeen and I came because your Mom really misses you, and your father, too, I bet." I kind of hung my head on that mouthful. "We gotta get these two back to town and we need their horses. You know where they stashed them, these *kîhkwahâhkêws*, these wolverines, these quick-hatches like the folks in Hudson Bay talk about all the time? The Cree folk got them pegged, alright."

"Yup," the boy said, "over in another cave. It's attached to this one, but off in there." He pointed to a dark end of the cave. "Indians marked it all up a long time ago, all the walls with animals on them. Some of them I've never seen. Later on I might live in here for a whole year, copying things down." He tipped his head and asked, "Wolverines? They drew them on the walls, too." His smile was as bright as a summer morning in spite of an ordeal lots of kids his age couldn't have handled.

After that, it was as sweet and smooth as eating lemon meringue pie. We had 'em bound and mounted on their horses and headed back to town. I sure hoped we wouldn't meet any of the posse on the way; I wanted Chase's Mom to see him first; and if you don't know the reason why by now, I'm not about to tell you.

But I'd see his father later, for sure. The paymaster.

A Dragoon's Adventure

The cowman Oliver Weddle sat his horse on a small hillock, looking out over his ranch, the grass running off to the hills, Texas itself stiffening his backbone as it always had. He tried again to count the help he'd need to get the ranch back in prime order after his return from the war, wishing that some of his command had come along with him when he separated from the service. They were good soldiers, good riders, and courageous and loyal to the duties; but had their own visions of search. Three foremen in a row had failed him and their mission, one or two of them he suspected had complicated issues on purpose. So glaring were the failures that they cost him a good deal of his money. Now he was contemplating what would happen if he did not get a good man for the job.

Even as his backbone stiffened again, hope still working him with its lures, he caught sight of an odd rider coming his way, ramrod straight in the saddle, commanding the horse, pride in the pair, but an unusual pride and seemingly an uncomfortable pride.

The rider was odd because of his manner and because he wore a strange hat, its brim swept to one side and up along his head, a long loop of leather twine hanging about his chest to catch that hat if blown off when riding. A saber's sheath and holsters for a rifle and an ax were strapped to his saddle, a definite portion of each weapon clearly visible. The saddle itself was different than a western saddle. Such equipment immediately set the rider off from the usual rider in the west, marking him as an object of attention and potential derision. A cardinal red shirt, scarred or stained where military chevrons once were attached, was filled by a rugged body, huge upper arms and prominent, wide shoulders. The man's neck was thick, tanned, muscled. Weddle suspected the man was not comfortable in the saddle but bore any and all his discomforts with command and control, like a poor cowpoke dancer challenged at a barn rally.

"Sir," the rider said on reining his horse in at Weddle's side, "I am one-time Sergeant Branwell Kirkness, late of His Royal Majesty's 6th Inniskilling Dragoons Cavalry Regiment, war my training ground and war my nature. Finding my pay cut after harsh service in India and South Africa, my comrades so treated likewise, I departed the military in 1865 and I am looking for a job riding herd here in western America. The chip I carry on my shoulder concerning my military treatment is most likely evident in all my outward manners and can be determined, by the most observant people, as roiling under my skin. But I am a hard and loyal subordinate when treated with respect and will protect with my life if necessary all trusts given unto me."

He stared into Weddle's eyes when he said, "Do I have a position in your employ?"

"That you do, sir," Weddle said, the iron up his back stiffer than ever, and hope as firm.

There, at that moment, began one of the great associations in Texas cow history.

Kirkness said to Weddle, upon being hired as foreman, "Tell me what you need done, but don't tell me how to do it."

"I need a crew to drive a herd of 3000 cows to Fort Gibson and merge them with two other herds for a drive up the Shawnee Trail to Abilene. I've heard they'll be 10,000 cows in the final push into Kansas. There's money to be made while the opportunity lasts."

"That I will do," Kirkness said, his voice as sure as a line sergeant's voice. "When is the drive to start?"

"In two days."

That evening former Dragoon sergeant and new BLB foreman Branwell Kirkness was in the Barrows Saloon, leaning against the bar, talking to one man who was a possible hire. "I don't expect promise from anybody, only duty from men with heart. Of course," he added with appropriate needling, "not all men have such heart. I am too particular to hire a slave or a roustabout or a lackey. I just want men. It may seem such a simple demand, but it has a lot at stake. Real men are rare when it gets tough."

"Yeh," said a voice from a nearby table, "how come the BLB hires foreigners wearing funny hats to be their top man? Ain't that a kinda funny hat?" A big, bony man, looking hard as a rock, stood up and faced Kirkness. "What is that hat, mister? Your mother make it for Christmas or did you bring it all the way from Inja with you?"

With one punch Kirkness dropped the big man beside the table. The big man did not move. Five minutes later he was still motionless. Stillness, sudden stillness in a noisy saloon, came with the mystery that silence has.

Kirkness eventually said, to all the cowpokes in the saloon, "I'm looking for real men, not flag mouths that can't take a punch. I wouldn't have that man now prone on the floor handling my wagon on a Sunday ramble. In India he would not have lasted one skirmish against the Gurkhas or the Sikhs at their worst. Nor would he have made his way against the Africans bent on freedom. If you want to measure men, measure me. I would guess that the prostrate figure there on the floor is typical of you westerners; all mouth and no guts for a long drive, or taking orders from their betters, or averse to good pay, real decent pay and a piece of the big pie, as the boss man has promised. How you ever did wrest the colony from the Mother country goes beyond my ken."

So convincing was Kirkness's approach that the following morning he arrived at the BLB Ranch with 11 men, and more on the way. The sun was shining on the small parade, with former sergeant Kirkness riding out front of the new hires, straight and upright in the saddle, his funny hat perched atop his head. Some of the new hires were battle-tested on the way to the ranch when Kirkness was openly challenged. He pummeled three men before dawn slipped up on them. Now, in the clear sunlight of morning, Oliver Weddle watched his new foreman bring a trail crew to the BLB. A sudden shot of surprise and happiness flooded his frame and he rode out to meet the men.

Weddle stood in his stirrups to get a clear look at his new crew. "Gentlemen," he said, "I am pleased to meet you. I trust you have met Sergeant Kirkness and know now who the real boss is. I too am a mere hireling here, but with a great project in front of us, with the promise of a great payday for all of us, we can complete our task." He pointed at Kirkness and added, in a voice full of will and determination, "That man will take us to Hell and back if that is what it will take, clear through the Oklahoma Indian territory. I don't doubt for a minute that he'll get us through and that some of you, wiser after the journey, will start your own business. There's room for all in this part of the land. The east is hungry for good beef, from Chicago to Philadelphia to New York City to Boston, Texas steaks have caused a craving. I don't know how long it will last, but let's get in on the feeding."

In the ranks a soft voice said, "Amen."

In the matter of two days a cook with trail experience was hired, a remuda assembled for herders and a remuda boss put in charge, assignments wagered between the men, and a partner system set in place. Kirkness was highly in favor of the partner system. "Stony, no matter where Clint Harkness goes, you be his pard. Keep your eyes open when it's your turn to do so, and he will do his in turn. The man who falls asleep at his watch gets the holy hell from me, and then some. And you've seen some of that and then some. I don't have time to fool around or play games this side of beef delivery. Be alert. Be aware. Be smart. It'll all come back on you."

At the outset of an Indian attack in the middle of Oklahoma, the Indians rode in against the herd in a double column, as if trying to split the herd and drive cattle off through whatever proved to be the weakest side, a maneuver none of the cowpokes had seen before.

"What the hell they up to, Cap'n?" one rider said. "I ain't seen them do this before."

Kirkness replied from horseback, "I've seen this before, in India, at the hand of the Gurkhas, some of the finest fighters in the world, and the meanest I've ever seen in action." He yelled to any herder close enough to hear him, "Fire on the right column. Concentrate on the right column. Obliterate the right column. Fire on the right."

He said it a dozen times.

Then, heedless of the onslaught and the odds, he swung head on at the left hand column and brought his rifle to bear on the column heading in on his herd and emptied the rifle. Then he blazed away with his six guns and saw several Indians fall from their mounts in succession. The raiders veered off from the left hand column as the right column suffered significant casualties as they were repelled by the herders, and the cattle in a mad turmoil it would take hours to arrest. The main attack, though, was stemmed in a matter of minutes and three other riders rode out and joined Kirkness in his continuing rush at the Indians.

Kirkness made a point of driving a couple of cows toward the retreating Indians, knowing it was cheap enough to buy some time by assuring they had meat for their meals. When the Indians were all driven off, including the few cows that Kirkness assured were in close pursuit of the fleeing braves, night came down on the herd as most of the herd was finally rounded up. Kirkness went on a regular night watch. He had done so since the drive first started.

Near midnight, from the edge of a small dip in the land, he heard the moans of a distressed person and found an Indian suffering from a serious wound. He managed to stop his bleeding, bind him with a piece of his shirt, and hustle him back to the chuck wagon where his cook could better treat and dress the wound. The cook was a good man at his trade and almost as good as any doctor in the area, and had no aversion to treating the Indian who was still unconscious.

"You know what this'n be like when he wakes full, boss. He won't be any less meaner'n he was afore. Too bad he won't git to know what you done for him. Want me to tie his hands?"

"Best do as you ask, Silas. Tight at each wrist but loose enough between them so he understands he's been left to have some use of his hands. We will try to communicate any way we can. Let us hope he has some understanding of the situation." Looking down at the brave, who was obviously a normally rugged individual, he added, "Poor bloke is not about to go too far in his shape. Set a bit of food where he can have it if he chooses. Keep trying to communicate any way possible." He went back on his watch for another hour and came back to sleep. In a matter of minutes, under a blanket and beside the wagon, he went to sleep.

Just as dawn broke over the plains, Kirkness was awakened by the coughing of the wounded Indian, who had risen on the other side of the wagon. The rope at his wrists allowed him to kneel, and then, with a struggle, stand upright. Kirkness pulled on his boots, went to the Indian, and put his hand on the bandaged wound. Then he set the food the cook has prepared at the feet of the man, taking a piece of dry beef for himself and chewing on it. Retrieving his blanket he put it about the Indian shivering in the morning light.

Silas the cook, already awake, said, "Boss, some of the boys be mighty upset at the kindness you've spent on the critter. They been shootin' at us and tryin' to make off with our pay stake 'n' that don't sit well."

Kirkness was back to his old self in a hurry. "Any man wants to change things, tell him to see me, Silas. I'll take care of his ailments too."

The story, the rest of what has come down to me, went something like this, with portions or snippets some of which I must have conjured up in my own way of telling it; but Kirkness, that late afternoon, rode off with the wounded Indian on another horse toward the far hills. The Indian sat a horse that Kirkness told the remuda boss to "get the one we can most spare."

Half a dozen riders watched the boss man ride off with the Indian still trussed up like he'd never get any place on his own. But somewhere out of sight of the herd and its riders, Kirkness untied the bound wrists of the brave who rode on ahead of him, turned on the crest of a small hill and held his hand palm upward. Kirkness did the same, the universal salute between warriors of the first line. The Indian rode down into a wadi and was out of sight and Kirkness, a sense of timing and circumstance working in his mind, sat his horse and waited.

He might have been waiting for a sign, an omen, any signal that his efforts, his belief in man, would have brought off a response of a similar nature. Most men would bet against him.

Kirkness stayed in his place, giving his horse a bit of water, watching for the evening star to give promise of night, hoping one harsh day would lead into one of clearer comfort and ease. Man, at his labors, at his wars, whatever the causes and the reasons, needed his rest. He clearly wanted his. This business he was into, the adventure in a new land, this liaison with a trusting owner like Oliver Weddle, had come like a reward to him, even though the costs might be high. He again hoped for the best in man, as he had often seen the worst in man ... on both sides of the fray.

It was at first a small illumination that came to him in the wavering shadows, from north of him, from where they were planning to drive the herd, right through country inhabited by Cherokee or Cheyenne or Arapaho. He could not tell the difference from one to the other if they stood in front of him at parade rest, but assured himself that they were as different as Gurkhas and Sikhs standing in the same formation, under the same colors.

The illumination grew, brightened, came on the obvious rise of a small hill hidden in darkness. It was, he knew, a signal, for the Indians could have gotten a lot closer to him. In the morning, he assured himself, other signs would be evident.

He hoped he had made peace for the time being.

He would like to do the job right for Oliver Weddle; trust was always part of his duties.

Beside the wagon, under the light of stars, the former Dragoon slept a deserved sleep.

Silas shook him awake. "Boss, coffee's up, biscuits on, shift change." And in a most condescending tone, said, "It looks quiet out there 'n' all the way back toward the risin' sun 'n' clear through to Montana up in front of us I'da bet." It was an affirmation of what the old soldier had done the night before.

Kirkness, with soldier skills still working his system, changed his socks, pulled on his boots in preparation for his day. When he rinsed his used socks and hung them on a pin on the wagon, he spotted the dried blood of the wounded Indian on the spokes of a wagon wheel and thought of the flames from the night before. "There," he said lightly, "was enough light for all of us."

Again, as it had so often happened, his whole life passed in quick review, as if a silent bugle had summoned his thoughts. "Call to Colors" came to him and "Reveille" and other bugle calls that were locked into his system. He remembered, coming this way, arriving at this place, the morning he walked through West Point and felt the ramrod spiking up his back. The military in him would, even in separation, carry him through. It had made him the man he was.

Oliver Weddle, of course, finished off the story as it had begun with him. Time and time again, in all his meetings with old friends and old comrades, in saloons, at card tables, at the spiked bowl at a now-and-then barn dance, said always that "Branwell Kirkness, late of His Royal Majesty's 6th Inniskilling Dragoons Cavalry Regiment, is the best herd driver I've ever known, the toughest man I've ever met, and the most trustworthy man that ally and foe can possibly know."

He told them all that Kicking Horse, a son of a Comanche chief, had cleared the way for Kirkness's herds for three years in a row. Not a shot was fired, not a cow was lost, though other drivers had their problems.

"The man's a soldier no matter what he wears," was often the way he said goodnight.

A Garden of Plenty

Monroe Boxler and Madeleine Solari were married in Independence, Missouri on the last day of May, 1870, Boxler separated from the army and Madeleine free of a despotic family to which she was more slave than daughter. All she ever wanted was her own garden and Boxler, on their first late night meeting when she slipped out of the house, promised her that she'd have her own garden if she married him and they'd go west, to a new opportunity for both of them.

That was the night of May 27th. On Monday, May 30th, she slipped out of the house for the last time. During the first week of June, they were west-bound in a wagon train. Neither one knew where they'd end up. During the whole trip, she dreamed about her first garden.

It was planted a year later in April, 1871 in north Texas, on a piece of land Boxler bought from a neighbor. A Confederate Army veteran, Boxler had become friends with another Confederate veteran, Morgan Drexel, who sold him 50 acres of land near the mountains. The couple built a small cabin on a special corner near a small stream; Madeleine thought it was idyllic, her husband thought it would be easier to protect in case of trouble, for trouble still moved on the land. There was free grazing land and there was the growing amount of land fenced in with barbed wire.

Madeleine did not like the "bob" wire that would hurt animals, but when cattle and other animals came into the early growths in her garden, she agreed to have it fenced in by her husband who adored her.

Boxler bought his wire from the general store in the nearest town. He went into the saloon to have a drink, and pause long enough to say hello to any friend who might drop in. He was nearly accosted by a couple of young toughs who had seen the wire in his wagon.

"You fixin' to wire off your spread, mister?" one of them asked.

Boxler, surprised by the question, but fully alert to the source, said, "It's for my wife's garden. She has some nice vegetables coming along and the animals have been getting into the garden. I've heard her some nights get out of bed and stand guard ready to move them off."

"Yah," replied the tough cowpoke weighed down by two side arms sitting like monsters on his hips, "that's what they all say."

Boxler, unarmed, used to young braggarts and their offensive introductions to an otherwise sane and calm situation, said, "Are you calling me a liar?"

The affronted young cowpoke spun about before his companion said, "He ain't carryin', Bobby. See that, don't you?"

Boxler, reading the young men again, said, "Are you saying that the deer don't get into my wife's garden and eat her crops?" He was still leaning against the bar, and in a corner of the room, smiling to himself, sat the owner of the general store where Boxler bought his wire, and a few other things. His smile broadened the more he looked at Boxler, the more he thought of purchased items that had landed in the Boxler wagon on other visits. His name was Griffin Attenborough.

The testy young cowpoke said, "Hell, yes. We ain't seen a deer all year when we hunted. The damned wolfs might have got them all." He laughed loud and added, "Yuh, I'm sayin' no deer get in that garden of yours in the next two days."

"If I bring in a deer in the next two of days and drop him at the door, will you keep quiet about the garden and the wire?"

Attenborough smiled again, a full and broad grin, and stood up and spoke to the whole room. His voice carried well in the room. "Morgan, that's one hell of a claim you're making. I'd like to see that myself. I've been out there myself and didn't get off a shot. No, siree, not a shot."

Attenborough's stature in the town just about carried anything he might say, even if casually, for everybody traded and did business with him … clothes, guns, ammunition, food of the strangest sort that ordinarily did not get to a chuck wagon but were reserved for the women of the area and their meal preparations. And he reflected again on the supplies Boxler had bought from his store.

Boxler, out of the "situation" with the young cowpoke, finished his drink, waved to Attenborough and then said to the young cowpoke and his pal, "See you gents in a couple of days … at the most."

At his arrival at home, Madeleine said, "How was your day in town? Did you get everything? My peas are up. Supper is baked potatoes and venison any way you like it." She hugged him a second time. Life was good.

After a delicious meal, Boxler thanked his wife with a kiss and taking his rifle off the wall rack, said, "I am going to get another deer."

"Oh, we have enough for almost a whole week," Madeleine said. There was a quizzical look on her face.

"Well, I made a promise in town, so if I get one I'll have to go back to town with it."

She laughed and said, "You hardly ever fail. You must be the best hunter in the whole west."

Boxler walked away from the house as evening shadows started to fall across the grass and climb the small rise their cabin was built on. The sun had disappeared behind western peaks earlier, there came night noises from the hills and out on the grass, and in the evening sky there soared a large bird he could not identify.

Boxler, too, thought life was good.

He sat behind a small frame of cast-off wood that was propped on both sides by branches off a tree, tested the wind direction, took a breath, and prepared to wait. Not an hour went by, the shadows in a full onslaught but on another mound the crest of the mound was clearly visible. He had planned all this almost a whole year earlier.

A shadow moved on the mound, and was familiar to Boxler who had placed his rifle over the top of the wooden frame in a homemade cradle. He eyed the shadow, squeezed the trigger and saw the shadow leap in the air, make a second jump and disappear into deeper shadows.

He walked back to the barn, tied his horse up to a small cart and rode out to where he had last seen the shadow disappear.

The deer was dead on the grass about 50 or 60 yards from where he hit it. With a sharp knife he carried in a sheath, he dressed the deer, carried the gutted remains in a large container and dumped them in the stream. The carcass of the deer was set on the back of the cart and he hung it well off the ground from a large branch of a tree near the cabin. It would be safe until morning.

The next day, after chores were done, he set out for town in his wagon, the deer in the back of the wagon. He went into the saloon, to the great surprise of everybody in the room, except for Griffin Attenborough who still carried the know-it-all smile on his face.

The two young cowpokes were amazed to see Boxler.

"Well, where's the deer?" the noisy one said.

"It's in the wagon out front. I wasn't sure what you wanted to do with it. I can deliver it if you tell me where to go, who to see."

Half the saloon customers rushed out to get a look and there in the back of Boxler's wagon was the dressed down deer almost as big as life. It was a good-sized buck with many points on its antlers.

Quick amazement and congratulations ran through the crowd and the noisy cowpoke said, "Oh, you can have it. I don't like venison, and that one looks awful tough with all them points on it."

"Not too tough to shoot," said a voice from the crowd.

Inside, still at his evening drink, Attenborough saw the vision that had been in his mind much of the night. In it he saw Boxler, from a large sack of salt he had bought at his store, mix much of it in the dirt around an old stump and put some of the salt on the stump, making it the first salt lick Attenborough had ever seen put up in such a manner.

But it worked, as did the "bobbed" wire around Madeleine's garden.

Breakheart Station Master

Deacon Almsbury wasn't an agent of God. He didn't come from Heaven, but came right up out of Hell ... and he was on his way this day to Breakheart Station. Clothed somewhat in cleric's black but far from the actual garb, Almsbury's true shape and dimensions were hidden. So were his weapons, cached in some fold of black cloth and often appeared mysteriously in his hands quicker than a pair of rabbits. Almsbury, it had been known for nearly a dozen years, ran ahead of himself, coming well in advance on wings of gossip, in headlines of weekly papers, and with riders who carried the word like a satchel on their saddle.

Once The Deacon visited a place, the impression stayed in place. Even the Cherokee Nation, all the villages in the territory, knew about him, talked about "The Man in Black, man with quick bullet, man shoot from shadow, man know death like brother."

His infamy ran wide and free.

Gus Turbit waited for the dust to rise from the road where the stagecoach would come over the hill about a half mile away. The replacement team was tethered in front of the station, ready to continue the incoming stage run to Axle Hill, the next stop.

An uneasy feeling came over him when he saw, down trail, the figure of a tall man on horseback racing toward him and his station of the Dewey Lines Route to Forever and Beyond. Turbit loved the sign saying those exact words painted up over the front door into the station where Maria had a pot of soup handy and a few loaves of freshly-baked bread, the table getting ready for passengers. He had painted the sign himself with a certain flair for the brush he'd found in his wrist.

The rider, he pondered woefully, would be here before the stagecoach, seeing how the horse was running full out. Turbit would rather have a few more guns just in case the rider was not good news in himself. He knew there was trouble due on the stage, with guns in the hands of The Deacon.

Turbit had been told that Deacon Almsbury would be coming in today; his horse, delivered a day earlier by a known friend of Almsbury's, Dasher Dixon, who said, "Hold the horse for The Deacon, and don't tell a soul he's coming in on tomorrow's stage, or else you'll be talking to the wrong end of The Deacon's gun ... or mine." The Peacemaker was in Dixon's hand with a spirited move and a scowl on his face.

That was enough for Turbit who didn't even tell his wife Maria that The Deacon was due in today. Maria had a way of blabbing out secrets ... but who could she talk to today if she knew anything at all?

There was nobody but him and the unknown rider still coming toward the station. The rider was almost close enough to hail, but the station master did not yell out a welcome.

He slopped another pail of water from the well into the trough, ready to tend the team he'd unhitch from the incoming stage. He loved the power of horses especially when they were teamed up, like the notable set ready and waiting for the transfer.

Bellcap, a big black who carried strength, beauty and command in his presence, was the lead horse on the replacement team and seemed anxious to get going, hoofing the earth into dust, shaking his kingly head. Turbit loved magnificence and saw it in Bellcap.

The station master, without taking his own meal off Maria's table, would tend the incoming team as soon as he could. "Well," he'd said in many a discussion, "that's my job, ain't it … taking care of horses? What else is there out here besides a good woman to take care of? Horses and women, they rank up there together on top of the pile." He'd snicker, in the company of gents, assured that Maria was not about, and add, "You put the horse first in some situations … but not in others." He said it in a way, with his eyebrows raised, that drew a round of laughter.

Never did he mention the care he gave to his secreted weapons, a pair of Colt revolvers and three rifles he had stashed around the station, hidden from prying eyes but readily available to him if needed … a quick move from just about any place in the station would produce a rifle in his hands, or the Colts he rarely wore at his regular duties. Each of those weapons received regular maintenance from Turbit and in less than six months of operation he had used a stashed weapon to thwart a few thefts of property, usually one of the horses, by a cowpoke gone broke at the card table, run out of town without his horse, and looking simply for a way to get home.

Nor did he mention the well, the one he had dug when so directed by the old Cherokee that he'd found wounded from a fall not far from where he now stood. He had taken care of the old one for close to a week. In return, Bent Claw had insisted there was water only at a certain point in the valley. He had heard of the white horseman searching for water and had laughed at his futile efforts.

But it was what drove Turbit in the first place: If he found water, and dug a well, he was guaranteed the Dewey Lines Route would build a station and he'd be the station master. Where directed by Bent Claw, Turbit found water at nine feet and walled the sides with rocks. He had his station, and his wife Maria came in on the second day of operation to do the cooking for hungry passengers on the roughest leg of the trip from the capital to Washington Heights, the end of the line at the Snake River.

The rider was a hundred yards away, slowed his horse, and finally pulled a big gray to a standstill at the water trough. "Okay to let him drink, ain't it?"

But it wasn't a question. It was like a boss talking to a hired hand.

Turbit had never seen him before, this big man, as tall in the saddle as he could remember a man sitting, an odd pistol on his belt, a mean look on his face as if he had just been stung by a hornet or, worse, a card shark on the other side of a big pot. But most significant was his left cheek, decorated with a black birth mark, circular, about an inch in diameter, with a growth of black hair in it as dark as a black beard. It twisted him sideways when Turbit looked at him, trying to size up all the points discernible, and make a lasting character study. As it was from that first look, the hairy birthmark promised to remain longest in the memory; it made Turbit uncomfortable, as if the man had noted that's what he kept looking at and would remember that stare.

Then the stranger turned Turbit's day upside down, when he said, "What time does The Deacon's stage get in? It's today, isn't it?" He looked off toward the hill on the incoming road, no sign of dust rising, no horses at a gallop, no driver trying to make the best of time. "I haven't got all the time in the world. He's coming today, right?" He kept patting his horse, a red mare, on the neck as she drank from the trough, and whispering words softly to her that Turbit could not hear.

At that moment, Turbit, lover of horses, fond of men who loved their horses like kin, forgot the man's strange and ugly birthmark and knew that he wholeheartedly liked the man.

And for a bare moment, the station master felt that fate this day had come to Breakheart Station in the person of this tall stranger.

That feeling allowed Turbit to say, "You know The Deacon? He expecting you to meet him?" He had the sudden realization that he could unfold the secret he'd kept to himself. "One of his men brought a horse for him yesterday, so that tells me he's due, and probably on the stage coming here pretty soon. I keep looking for the trail dust to rise out there on the road. He expecting you, The Deacon?"

"He ought to be," the stranger said. "He owes me and mine for a whole lot of misery, and I aim to set things straight on the account." His stare was loosed down the trail behind him the way some folks allow things to catch up to them in times of measurement or accountability. Turbit, working with the public on numerous jobs, had seen such contemplation on many occasions; men sworn to avenge a serious grievance.

Hearing the tone of the stranger's voice at its clearest, Turbit no longer noticed the strange birthmark, as if the man had clouded it over with his determination of squaring some past account ... not yet brought to terms. "Should I expect trouble here when he comes? Should I hide my woman? She's had her share of problems since she joined me." He looked the stranger in the eye and said, "I'm not too swift on such accounts myself, but I'd like to know who you are, what your name is. Would you tell me so as I'll have a grasp on this matter looking like it's coming my way and me with not much to say about it getting done or not getting done."

Now the birthmark appeared again to Turbit as the stranger seemed to be mulling things around in his head, his eyes moving out to the trail and back again. Turbit, in a quandary, wondered in what manner it had disappeared because he could not bring it back immediately, the way it had happened with him only moments earlier. Did the folks the stranger mentioned not see the birthmark any longer? Had they forgotten it in time? Because of love? Were siblings or parents conditioned to it? Forgotten it was there after the first shock? What kind of accounts had to be squared between this man and The Deacon?

"I could ask a hundred questions," Turbit said.

"Don't bother," the marked man said. "My name is Dave Kershon. Six months ago The Deacon set fire to my parents' house and they died in the fire. I was off in the army and got out right away and been looking for him. Almost caught up to him in Cuttersville, but he was a day gone when I got there. I think he knows I'm looking for him."

Kershon was off his horse. He was six feet tall, wore a gray Stetson the sun and rain and trail dust had darkened considerably, and the rim flopped in a haphazard way as though he did not care how it looked. On his belt was a single Colt, perhaps an army model. It was not worn the way The Deacon most surely wore his weapons, or any other fast gunman. It also was not the kind of weapon fast gunmen usually carried. He wore no spurs on his boots because they were some type of army issue. The pants, showing wear, had faded yellow Union stripes down the legs.

All in all, Turbit thought, Kershon was apparently out of his class opposing The Deacon. Anger and revenge might not carry the load for him.

He remembered quickly, as if testing himself, where his own weapons were hidden about the station. With a quick look he saw two places he could get to in a decent hurry if he had to if a gunfight broke out when the stage came in. With a scene in his mind, he imagined how he could be of use to Kershon.

Kershon's head snapped when he heard a yell and the two men looked up and saw the dust rise on the road and the stagecoach cross the brow of the small hill. It would be at the station in a short time. He pulled the weapon from its holster, checked the load and replaced the weapon in the holster.

Turbit was convinced again, looking at the weapon, that Kershon stood little chance of doing in The Deacon. He looked about the station yard, refreshing his memory ... just in case he had to help the man who already looked to be on the short end of the deal.

He yelled to Maria standing in the doorway, "You put the pot on the table, Maria, and go down in the hole right quick. Right quick, you hear me! Right quick!"

She disappeared from sight.

Kershon tied his horse off at the side of the trough and walked to the open part of the station, the sun in his eyes.

Turbit shook his head at that move, wondering if Kershon really had been through the war and how he had searched for The Deacon for half a year and stayed alive. He'd have been known by the birthmark no matter where he went, and he probably could not hide out in many places if he tried. Turbit saw him squint as he looked toward the east and the stagecoach coming with the sun and then Turbit's eyes caught sight of another riding coming in from the west and he recognized The Deacon's friend, Dasher Dixon, galloping toward them.

Rushing to his replacement team, Turbit brought the team right to the front of the station, ready to hitch them up in the exchange. The stage was nearly on them, and Dixon, too, coming up the trail. Kershon seemed oblivious to all but the stagecoach, his eye steady on it, not noticing Dixon at all.

The door to the station was wide open and Turbit knew his wife was hidden in the crawl hole he had dug to escape any threat. The replacement team, with Bellcap standing like a monument at the lead, stood ready for the transfer.

Kershon had not moved from the position he had taken, in the center of the station yard.

The stage driver, veteran of many trips on the line, and more than once with The Deacon as a passenger, realized that the man standing in the center of the open area was here for a showdown with The Deacon. He had seen it before ... and had seen men go down trying to face The Deacon. He saw the other rider, off to one side of the corral, dismount and leave his horse's reins dragging on the ground. He assumed the scales had been tipped in The Deacon's favor in the coming fray ... just as Turbit did.

The stage was pulled short of its usual stopping place by the driver.

The Deacon, clothes black as Hell could be without fire, stepped down from the stage, eyed the man in the center of the area, saw Dixon at the corner of the corral, and the harmless station master standing by the water trough.

One hand of The Deacon was clearly visible as he moved it slowly out from his side. His other hand was hidden in the folds of his black clothes.

The driver stayed in place, up on the boot of the wagon.

Bellcap nickered either from his impatience to get going or his noting the odor of the incoming horses.

The Deacon said, "Who are you? You the guy been looking for me? You the one with the hairy mark on his face? Before you go down, tell me your name and why you're looking for me."

"I'm Kershon and you killed my parents when you burned down their home over in Bridger when I was away in the army. You burnt them to death for no reason and I'm here to make up for murder."

"Oh," The Deacon said, "is that so?" and he moved his exposed hand to draw attention to it being empty, and Turbit saw motion beneath the black cloak and knew he had a gun in that hand.

He yelled to Kershon as he dove behind the water trough, "Look out behind you."

Kershon spun to look behind him.

The Deacon's hand came free with a weapon in his hand, and Turbit, from the other side of the trough, came to his knees with a rifle as The Deacon took aim at the dumbfounded Kershon drawing his old army weapon to fire at Dixon who already had a revolver in his hand.

When The Deacon fired two rounds at the spinning Kershon, one hit and killed the magnificent Bellcap who fell immediately to the ground, and the other shot raced off into the air.

Turbit screamed at the sight of Bellcap falling down in his traces, stood with the rifle on his hip and unloaded half a dozen rounds at The Deacon. Surprised at firing from the harmless station manager, The Deacon crumbled in place, and Dixon, not yet getting off a round in the excitement, grabbed his horse at the sight of The Deacon on the ground, leaped into the saddle and rode away, down the trail.

Kershon, not yet having fired a round from his old weapon, stood still in the middle of the yard, as the driver urged the team forward a bit, and yelled to his other passengers, "It's all over folks. You can get down now. Maria will have grub on the table. We have 15 minutes. The Deacon ain't going anyplace with us."

Bounty for a Sheriff

Bearded Max, mean as a barn full of peccaries, was never seen smiling as though he was judging the whole world all at one time and finding it wanting, spoke harshly, as always, to Marshy Barrett, one of the 7-Ten hands. "Everythin' in place, Marsh?" He said it the way boss men don't trust any minions under their wing and are quick to place blame for all faults thereafter. "You sure of that?" Max had a way of resettling his shoulders when he was talking to most fellows and it was meant to make them afraid that Max could at any minute slam them on the side of the head. None of them had seen Max use his gun, but his reputation was not lacking on that point.

"Wanna go see?" Barrett said, tired of Bearded Max already and it was only six in the morning, the day out in front of him like there was little promise coming.

"Don't sass with me, Marshy. I ain't in the mood."

"Hell, Max, I ain't ever seen you in no mood other'n what you got spinnin' now."

"Answer me, dammit."

"Yup," Barrett said. "Two men in the last two cars, tucked in behind some hay. Nobody saw them get up in there 'cause it was cave-black all night, no stars, no moon, nothin'."

"Why not 'nother car?"

"We checked it again, by that water stop near Closet Canyon just like you said. Best one for doin' what we can on most of the line for 50 miles or so. At least up to the Shady Valley water stop. Last two cars are 'bout out of sight of the rest of the train when gettin' water. Third car last ain't like that. But there's more'n 60 head in the two cars. Maybe 70. Nobody but us knows the way out of the canyon, and we got enough brush and wood piled up in there to start a forest fire if we had a few more trees in the way. They won't find anythin' if they come back to look."

Bearded Max, setting up a puzzled look on his face, said, "Who you got up in there?"

"Barnesy 'n' Pepper Don in the last 'n' the two new boys in the next last car."

"Didn't I pick two good uns, them two?"

"Sure did, Max, 'n' they can shoot like Belle Starr was pullin' the trigger if we was ever to need it. We're lucky we keep this up, no shootin' 'n' we get rich and they ain't hardly any work to it. I took another turn through the big cave we found and it's still okay. We can get 60, 70 or more head through there in no time, like they was greased. Like greased pigs, I swear."

As it was, for the purposes of this tale, one of the like Belle Starr shooters, no past proof about where or what he'd done in this here life, no papers, no starry badge, was none other than Drop-two Donahue, an imported lawman from Locust, California, a one-time comrade of Sheriff Wick Dubois of Barstow in the Vermont Cavalry in the Great War between the State. In Barstow rustlers had been spoiling and spilling the profits of other people's incomes in a variety of maneuvers and operations, most of which were at least novel in application. A new type of criminal was on the land and making waves, like stealing right out of cattle cars after the long haul herding from southern grass was accomplished by others.

It was to Dubois credit, and surprise, that he could say, "Now at last we have outlaws who do a bit of thinking and planning a crime instead of just plain shooting their way through people to get something for free." Sometimes it appeared that the sheriff was talking to his dog Sugar, sharing a bit of conversation, the dog never far from the sheriff. A keen observer, a local, if attentive, realized that Sugar probably collected the scent of every horse and person close enough to separate, and kept it in his arsenal of memories.

The bank at Lucky's Strike, up in the foothills, was the first crime of the sort that caught Dubois's attention. Lucky's Strike was up in the middle of country of rock slides and eruptions of sections of mountains, and now and then a touch of an earthquake rumbling like a small ocean wave across the whole region. It was natural cover-up that played a great part in the bank robbery, where a small blast under the bank dropped the poorly-protected vault down through the floor into a tunnel dug from the adjoining building and in which the vault door was easily blown off by a small blast people thought was another of the area rumbles ... until the bank was opened in the morning.

The new train robberies were rustling in a new way. Bearded Max, supposedly to the crew, had come up with it when he saw a long freight train getting water and wood loaded at a few railroad stops coming out of Abilene, Kansas and heading east. Already tired of bullets too close in what he called live rustling, he looked for other avenues of quick income. He did not have too many opportunities, but from those that came his way he took all that he could, as quick and clean as possible.

At close range, it would become obvious that Bearded Max, no other name available for him, was not the top dog in the group; someone versed in mechanics, explosives, topography and geography, human nature and scheduled activities, loose ends that people often let go of, inattention of others to detail, ran the operation: a Mr. Big who ran the show and who kept laid back all the way through to riches in one manner or another.

This current cattle theft directly from a train was the third such theft of cattle near Barstow, along the Kansas border.

The on-board rustlers had a simple task when the train was stopped for water and the latest heist; out of sight of the engineer and oiler, they simply dropped one of the off-side door ramps, which opened the way for cattle to exit the two cars, get driven quickly into a wide-mouth cave or some place under immediate cover and be pushed on to a previously selected site. None of the train crew saw anything of the actions, which were discovered in two earlier efforts only at the train's arrival at destination.

Bearded Max figured he'd have at least one more chance at the same watering stop and a few chances at two other sites he had explored, and then that tactic would have to be forgotten. He'd have to develop a new way at easy living; that's what he said to the crew doing the dirty work.

The crew believed Bearded Max was the big man of the operation, had all the ideas, and knew what was going on with the law, within the law.

Drop-two Donahue, once the heist was completed and he was lead to the select gathering site for a larger herd collection, and eventual shipment east, reported his find on the sly to Sheriff Wick Dubois, Barstow sheriff.

Drop-two Donahue was convinced Bearded Max did not have the brains to conceive the operation and its needed connections. He was right on the money on that, but had no additional information on who was at the top of the tree.

Dubois, in turn, thought Donahue was correct about a secret boss, possibly someone from the local area, but few names came into his mind as possibilities. "We need some good connection to the top dog, Drop-two," he'd said, "a trail if not to his door, at least enough to start a list of possibles."

Donahue, in his own assessment, said, "They're different, Wick, like they not only don't want a shoot-out if it can be helped at all, but take every precaution to avoid one. That to me is the smart decision and it must be made at the top; murder, if it comes up in one of their jobs, makes it tougher to get away from. Hard to avoid in the long run. Besides, the big dog might find it tasteless as well as useless. Think about that. It might start a list for you; it might place some character into a crook, if you get my drift. Who out here has not and would rather not use the gun, legally so to speak, to keep or protect his property?"

"That's something that never dawned on me, Drop-two. Most anyone I know would fight tooth and nail for family and property. It goes with the territory and always has. I've known women fight like the fires of Hell was in them and no quit as long as they could breathe."

For a few moments he mused on the idea. "You get what information you can from wherever and I'll look at those folks in the region in that way you spoke about. Who knows, maybe we'll fight novel crooks with novel looks."

Donahue, with the rest of the rustling crew, was directed a few weeks later to a meeting place in a small wayside cabin tucked into a shady valley on the Kansas border, where Bearded Max explained the next cow train theft. It would be at a new location with practically the same layout as the latest Barstow theft, except the rustled cattle would be driven off through a ravine adjacent to the water and fuel stop.

And Sheriff Wick Dubois spent one afternoon later in the week looking at every townsman who passed by his office and went into the general store or the saloon. On the porch of his office and jail he sat on a comfortable bench, leaning back against the building like he was enjoying a good rest and taking in a great day of sunshine, his pet dog Sugar, as always sitting beside, little making the dog budge except a command from the sheriff.

Under his tipped sombrero Dubois's eyes did not miss a single person passing by, some yelling hello or waving at him from carriage, horseback or afoot. He knew them all ... all knew him.

His list of possible suspects was in this manner underway and, surprisingly right at the top, his first entry was none other than the dual-interested banker and rancher, Douglas Hetherton, his spread near as wide as the river was long, and the bank holdings deeper than his pockets could ever hold. Hetherton, it was known, had never pulled the trigger of a gun in anger, retribution or any kind of gain. Apparently everything he did was by the book, the legal book, though his rewards and gains came with high marks and greater riches for a mighty powerful man.

But Dubois said "no" to his possible connection even though no shot had yet been fired in any of the new, strange crimes. The amount of cattle put on trains by Hetherton interests was a common note in Barstow, for all the counts were logged by varied interests, sellers and buyers and accountable counters of such interests attending the loadings.

But Drop-two Donahue had raised a bubble of interest in the sheriff, so on a hunch he telegraphed a friend who was associated with the receiving yard in Chicago asking for counts on the Hetherton deliveries for the past year, and the telegrapher was warned not to breathe a word of the sheriff's outgoing and incoming messages. "A word of this gets loose in town, Harland, and I'll come after you with a whip. Bet on it." He saw the fear rise in the telegrapher's face; he knew the man thoroughly.

Dubois was surprised by the answering message.

The figures did not match; the receipts of arrival were almost twice the amounts loaded on trains in the Barstow yards. It was possible that the surplus was on the up and up, but Dubois had never heard of any other location from which Hetherton shipped his stock.

It was enough to go looking for answers; on the sly, of course. He enlisted Drop-two Donahue in that search. There was no response from him in three days. And when his horse ran into town, without rider, without saddle, Sheriff Dubois and Sugar went looking for Drop-two, Sugar on the scent of his horse. Dubois knew the dog would get him as close as possible; he'd have to finish it off.

Sugar was unerring in his search, heading out of town along the river, and then taking an abrupt turn up into the foothills and into a rocky crevasse. When Sugar circled aimlessly a few times on a rocky surface, and the sheriff knew he had lost the track of the horse, he pulled an old bandana of Donahue's from his pocket, one that had been in his desk at the office.

Sugar stuck his nose into the air, circled about, sniffed several times and then lit off for the far end of a rocky cliff. At a break in the cliff face, at a fissure wide enough to accept a man, he stiffened, all at attention. Dubois dismounted and started searching the area, eventually calling out his friend's name: "Drop-two, can you hear me? Drop-two, you hanging in here someplace? We followed your horse's scent back here, me and Sugar. Can you hear me?"

The clatter of a stone came from the crevice in the wall, and then a second stone sounded. But no voice called out.

Dubois clambered into the crevice; found his old pal beat all to a near pulp, one leg broken, one arm broken, and blood drying on much of his shirt. In one hand he held a small stone, in his able hand, and it suddenly rolled out of his hand and down the slanted surface. The sound carried. He was unconscious.

The sheriff got Donahue back to Barstow and the doctor. When his breaks were set, and he found his voice and lucidness, he told Dubois how a new hire had recognized him and the gang kicked the hell out of him and left him for dead. And he clearly recalled Hetherton saying, "No guns. No shots. Just beat the crap out of him and leave him someplace he can't get out of. Time will take care of him. Make it look like an accident, a bad encounter with an animal, a fall, but no gunplay. Make sure you all understand what I mean."

During the night he put Donahue in the last cell in the jail. There were no other prisoners, but Dubois stood guard all night. In the morning he deputized a dozen men, two who stood guard at the jail and not a soul was to be admitted until Dubois came back to the jail.

The sheriff and his ten deputies set up outside the bank waiting for it to open. When Hetherton rode up on his horse he was arrested, handcuffed and taken to jail. Two additional deputies were assigned to the jail, and Dubois and the balance of the deputies set out for the Hetherton ranch.

Without a single shot fired, all the bunkhouse occupants of the 7-Ten spread were brought back to jail, all trussed or handcuffed, each one sat on his own horse, and all firearms confiscated. Bearded Max, to nobody's surprise, was amazed at the change of circumstances.

Three days later, the bank still closed, the jail full to capacity just before the trial was to start, the whole mess ended up in an up-and-down trial that lasted less than two hours in front of the territorial judge. The guilty verdict was brought in on all those arrested except two hands who were late comers, but not the one who had fingered Drop-two. He was given three extra years in the penitentiary for pointing out the lawman to the gang.

The guilty were shipped off to the penitentiary, Drop-two was rehabilitated and sent on his way back to California, and the tunnel under the back was filled in and completely sealed against further entry. The bank, properly administered, was turned over to a committee of townsfolk who would run it until they selected a new president of the bank.

And Sheriff Dubois commenced sitting in front of his jail for another four years, with Sugar at his side, his tail continuously wagging.

It was good bounty for a man and his dog.

Colum Twyne's Last Leg Up

Not everything is as it seems. Sheriff Colum Twyne had heard that said a number of times, and here he was being the proof of the saying. He was hoping it was a true observation in this case.

This was it, he figured as part of his reasoning; "I'm 49 years old and I feel like I've been out here chasing this dude for my whole life as sheriff. Now he's shot my horse out from under me in the last bit of daylight. He'll be waiting for me at dawn, that rifle waiting to smoke again. It's damned sure he don't want to go back with me, not to Treasure Hills, not to that mob again, the one I kept off his neck a few nights ago. I can't rightly remember if it was a week ago or a hundred years ago, I'm getting plain tired."

He had extricated his leg from under the horse with some hard work, found it not broken, and knew he was lucky.

"I have to move and I can't move the horse, so I'll have to cut the saddle loose and hide it someplace in the dark. Can't stay here. This hombre Crostley said he'd do me in, even after I kept the mob off him. He was hard as ever saying, 'I swear, Twyne, I'll get you before they hang me.' Can't let him do that. Lucky I didn't break my leg when my horse went down. Maybe he meant to shoot the horse and not me. Make it real tough for the old man. We'll see."

He thought over his whole situation; what he'd done, where he'd been, the troubles that came to him on the job and somehow went away as he continued his work, drawing on a reserve that had not yet failed him. A sudden thought emerged, and he whispered the condemnation onto the ground beneath his mouth: "Maybe it is time to quit."

He didn't believe what he had just said; it sounded as if somebody else was speaking for him.

His rifle was intact, he had a canteen half full of water, one piece of dried meat left, a chunk of hardtack, but no coffee pot, and no coffee anyway. But he was alive; he had a chance. The old squaw woman who had brought him back from a bad wound way in the past, sounded her voice again: "Don't hide where him hunting you think you hide. Hide where Indian hide – in the open. Hide in the open, not behind tree or rock, not in bushes, in the open." She walked away as he turned his head and when he looked back again she was gone. For ten minutes he couldn't see her from where he lay in front of the cave. She had gone. Disappeared. He saw nothing and heard nothing even listening with an acute ear near the ground. Ten minutes later, like a spirit, she rose from behind a log mere feet from him, a smile on her face covered with dirt where she had nestled it on the ground, motionless for those ten minutes.

She exhibited a sly smile and said, "Where I hide Lakota call me *Winuȟčala ekta ahaŋȟi*. You call me Old Woman-in-Shadow."

In the darkness so that Crostley couldn't see him, couldn't see how tiredness showed in his face, in his eyes and the drop of his chin, in the constant way he lightly shook his head in disbelief that he had walked into a trap, letting the bad guy get off a single shot in the last bit of daylight.

"I made a mistake," he muttered. "I should have waited a couple of minutes more before I moved out of that gully. Well, too late now, horse out of the barn and dead as a door knocker waiting for company."

With a gentle hand he patted the dead horse and said, "You've been a good mount, boy. A good mount." It was the best testament he could give to the animal at the time.

He lugged the saddle for 30 or 40 feet, dropped it down, and dragged it another 50 feet toward the small copse of trees around a few boulders, thinking the boulders way in the past had rolled downhill from the higher level to get stopped here by trees so many generations ago. It would be very difficult for him to leave or discard his Cheyenne Rig saddle that Collins Brothers made for him. It would be as hard as losing his horse, but if he could barter or trade it for his life, it would be worth it; the horse had been so taken. He recalled the first time he rode on it, up on a horse with green-yellow fire in his eyes, and was called Tabasco.

At least another 100 feet from that cover of sorts he let go of the saddle and it sank to find its best resting position in a proper riding position, horn upright, fenders spread, as if on the back of a horse. The voice of Woman-in-Shadow returned, in a whisper, "Remember what squaw say. Hide where Indian hide."

Colum Twyne was a good listener; had always been a good listener. His grandfather's stories hung in his mind as if they had been spoken at the back end of a wagon only the day before, heading out of Winslow's Barn and crossing later that day the first railroad tracks he had ever seen, the rails running into a single point way up the line, the sun flashing on the rails until they became, in his eyes, a single arrow of light. The old gent, sitting with him at the back end of the wagon, noting the wonder in his grandson's eyes, he said, "They aren't that close the way they look way up there, Sonny. They just look that way. Same distance apart up there as they are right here, almost the width of the back end of a pair of oxen. It's all in how you look at things, know what they're supposed to be even so far off. You best remember what I say about how things supposed to look even if they don't."

Twyne heard the voice of Woman-in-Shadow as a quick add-on to his grandfather's advice.

Leaving his saddle in the tall grass, he dragged himself through the grass toward the trees, now and then rolling on the ground, flattening the grass. When he reached the tree-line, he went on through the site, veered off to his right and went back out on the grass; he did not walk upright the whole way.

He felt luck hanging around his person, standing by. The moon was still hidden behind a mass of clouds and off to the east he could see that moon penetrating small breaks in the clouds. Then he saw a vast break in the clouds and he lay down on the grass.

The moon broke loose in the first big break in the clouds and yellow moonlight shot down on the grass as if a torch had been thrown into the darkness. Twyne kept as motionless as possible, and began his patient wait by counting his breaths. It put him to sleep for a few hours, aware at times that the moonlight lit up much of the landscape, including where he was. Did only upright figures throw shadows, have shade at their feet, and become part of something else? Night sounds from the prairie, which he had long treated as a kind of personal music, pleasant company for the most part, came from the copse of trees, from the high tree line off to the west, and from a canyon down the line where life echoed in the night as though it was coming through a funnel ... the echoed signals of birds, coyote calls, grunts of a sow, and an unknown wild critter making a demand on territory.

A lone thick and dark cloud, black as a bundle, had drifted in from somewhere in a wind and from good providence at the moment. The yellow torch went out as if a generous hand had closed down on it.

Twyne almost let out a sigh of relief, but managed to hold it back. Silence was precious in so many ways. Woman-in-Shadow could be listening, and an echo of her words came on a slight lift of air, his education never complete: "Man talk with his feet. How he push horse under him. How he answer crow on a dead branch he cannot reach or a hawk on a soft wind he cannot feel. How he hears magic in water that touch all things living."

At that exact moment he heard at one ear, the one stuffed against the warm earth and grass and which he had not moved for what seemed hours, the single tromp of a boot. One foot came down on the earth. One boot! It could only be Crostley on the move, on foot as he now was, and aware that his pursuer had taken this new tact in the search. And he was being hesitant in his turn at searching, stealthy as an Indian.

Twyne held his breath, the rifle gripped in his right hand, trigger tight against his finger, the barrel of the weapon pointing back toward the way he had come ... and to where he had trampled the grass with the saddle, the saddle still sitting there but perhaps not visible to Crostley.

An abrupt, harsh curse, with an attempted mute pressed upon it, lifted on the darkness and was only feet from him. Twyne did not move his head. He did not look up. He did not breathe but slightly through his nose, holding to as much silence as he possibly could. Crostley must have stubbed his toe on the saddle, or a rock, or found an insect in his eye or in his ear. Twyne thought about his own ears ... one accessible to a flying insect, one totally available to a whole ant colony. He had been bitten several times in the last hour, prone on the ground, the grass and earth in his face. Time moving on as slow as the seasons, or a drive on the Red River route.

A foul odor came on the air and Crostley, he remembered, had not been near any free flowing water in the time he had been pursuing him.

If he could smell him, from feet away, on the gentle drift of warm air, a dozen animals must know he was out here on the grass ... and him too.

Animals could run away from an odor ... or rush to it.

Crostley's next trod down on the earth was taken ... and the sound of it advanced into Twyne's ear, the one on the ground. The air caught up in his lungs was building its pressure, and Twyne feared to let it go and feared to hold it back. Any sudden move on his part, voluntarily or involuntary, could get him dead in a hurry.

From far off in his senses Woman-in-Shadow spoke one more time: "He not see you lose a step. If he turn around he might catch up two step. Scare him quick. Take next step away."

It was done that quickly.

From his position, sensing where Crostley was standing near him in darkness, Twyne fired a round from his rifle, rolled quickly to his left, heard and saw the flash of Crostley's rifle only ten feet away and fired three fast rounds, rolled again, and came to a kneeling position, the rifle at his shoulder, his finger compressed on the trigger, his eyes seeking any silhouette, any sign, of Crostley.

The cry of pain came first, a scream that set off across the grass, with a curse following it as Crostley's rifle hit the ground with a soft thud and then a heavier thud as Crostley also hit the ground; "Damn you, Twyne! Damn you!"

At that moment Sheriff Colum Twyne suddenly realized that he'd been hit in the leg. He couldn't let Crostley know he had been wounded also.

"I'm hit real bad, Twyne. You got to help me."

"Where's your horse?"

"At the edge of those trees. I tied him off there."

Twyne said, "I'll go get him after I take your rifle and side arms. Then I'll get you back to a doctor." He paused and offered his last promise, "And back to jail, too."

With a bit of pain from his own wound, he retrieved his prisoner's rifle, took his side arms, and hid them near the trees when he untied the horse and brought him back to Crostley still hurting on the grass. He brought the horse close to Crostley, placed a rope about the horse's front legs to hobble him for a short time. Thinking about his situation, and not wanting to give Crostley another chance, he walked off a short way into the darkness and put his own weapons down on the grass.

With some difficulty Twyne managed to get Crostley across the back of the horse, looped his hands and feet to a length of rope passed under the horse, retrieved his own weapons, and mounted the horse in front of his prisoner.

Only when he was mounted did he say to Crostley, "You got me, too, in the leg, bad enough to make me think on it, not so bad that I can't do my job."

He gave no more explanation.

The two of them, both in pain, rode into Treasure Hills later in the day, and Crostley, and the sheriff, were both treated by the doctor … in the jail they had so recently left, Sheriff Colum Twyne thinking it seemed like yesterday when he started his pursuit, and knowing that he had come close to losing his leg, and perhaps his life, somehow promising himself that he had thrown his last leg up on a sheriff's work.

A Prairie Christmas Wish

They were lucky that the mule lasted long enough to haul in all the firewood from the forest, before he fell dead in his tracks. And there was little chance that there'd be any presents for the children, two boys. The snow had drifted in some places as high as 8-10 feet, and the path to the barn was treacherous when any wind was blowing. Gerard Fiddler knew he'd have to walk with a shovel to be sure he'd make it out and back, the snow drifts moving, falling, shutting off what was almost a tunnel at some points. He hoped he didn't have to try it again before the storm stopped.

At the stove his wife Muriel prepared another meal of venison and bread, the stove hot and keeping a sense of warmth about them, her and him and the two boys that were still tight under a mixed cover of blankets, old flour bags, winter coats, a few furs he'd traded for. They could stay there for the day if they wanted to, Christmas on the doorstep, one day away.

She had one wish.

Camden Prescott, Gerard's friend, had been here in late September, setting up the wood supply against one side of the cabin, covering much of it with a canvas from the old wagon buried by snow behind the barn. Good old Prescott, who had pulled Gerard wounded from the field at Gettysburg, making sure the doc fixed him, and who had journeyed out here on his own dream and heard Gerard's name in town and looked him up. Prescott would keep an eye on him and the family while he was in the area. Prescott was always on the way to someplace; as he'd say, "Over the rise, and down the skies."

The two days on the wood stacking and covering had been an exhaustive effort and Prescott had made Gerard do his regular chores while "this hired help" does the wood pile. He went at it with a ferocious energy, pausing only for water and a lunch of prairie chicken and beans and bread.

"Muriel," he'd said a few times, "you handle the skittle and the knife better than any woman I ever met, I swear and dare." She'd blushed each time, another man in the house for a short spell, a different outlook on things, her hoping that Gerard would make a good stand against the coming winter. The last one had been difficult. She had high hopes for the next one.

Now, in its ferocity, it was here, and she was as thankful as Gerard was about the wood piled against the side of the cabin, enough for the worst winter. She had wondered, at first, as Prescott took down a section of the side wall and put it back up, but knocked it in place from the inside, like another door.

"Why do that, Prescott, put those boards in backwards?"

She was all quizzical until Prescott said, "You can get to the wood right from here if you have to, if the winter is fierce you don't even have to go outside. That's why I'll cover the pile up with the canvas off the old wagon."

"The cold will come in as bad as ever," she had said, shivers running on her arms, Gerard nodding at the same time but saying nothing.

"I saw it done in a miner's place in Montana. It's a good trade-off for a day's worth of firewood, wouldn't you say, in a way?" He smiled that broad grin of his, his eyes lit up, asking for an agreeable answer.

Prescott was always thinking of people, of friends, and she decided he was a real good friend.

Now she knew, as the wind was kicking up again, that Gerard wouldn't have to venture outside for wood or anything ... at least not too soon. They had flour and beans in the house and a bucket of oats and there was a cache of meat frozen in the box by a window. It was as simple as the access to the woodpile and offered a good trade-off, as Prescott had affirmed.

She only worried about Christmas and something she could make for the boys, but she'd been so busy with the storm on them and worries about Gerard and his state of mind. More than once, looking at the boys sleeping under a pile of whatever, Gerard had said, "What did I come out here for? Why'd I drag you, Muriel? You're the best woman I ever knew."

She worried about that part of Gerard, worried that it might break loose the small chink in his resolve. He was her man and she'd stick with him through it all ... had done so on several occasions and was apparently at it again, the wind moaning again. But she gave thanks that the roof was covered with snow.

"It's part of winter protection," Prescott once explained, "like bears look for when they go to sleep for winter. Once I saw a bear go into a cave up there in Montana and pile up snow from the inside across the entrance to the cave, so nothing could get in there in the winter and disturb his sleep. That's the most natural protection from snow itself, using it against itself. The Eskimos way up in Canada make their little houses out of it, and crawl in deep and go to sleep."

For the few days Prescott was there, helping them out, he told stories about everything he had seen. The boys were in awe of him and the stories, coming to them from a man who they believed had been every place and seen everything there was to see. He'd been on the great river and two of the great lakes up north of them, and in the war with their father and had seen the oceans on both ends of the country and told it all … in two days, even as he worked like a beaver gnawing down a new home out of the forest and "taking the prize right under your eyes."

"Isn't there a woman in your life?" she dared to ask another time. Gerard was upset at that, but Prescott said, "So far, for me, it's been one woman, and that's Mother Nature at her best and at her worst and I figure I ain't been denied and she never lied."

Muriel looked up at that, the questionable look on her face, and he hurriedly replied, "Not that she. Not to me." And the chuckle touched them both.

Muriel loved how he'd rhyme things when finishing up a story. It pleased her mightily, and she soon realized, in the two days, that he knew it too. He was a most handsome man, with blond hair that sat like a ball of cotton tight and curly on his head, blue eyes that could not tell a lie to anybody on the face of the Earth, muscles that showed on him from wrists up to hidden bulges, and music in his voice every time he spoke. Muriel knew he must have been swayable with some women despite what he said.

But the two days of Camden Prescott were long over, winter was atop them with its week-long fury, and no stopping in view. The aroma of baking bread filled the room, and she looked up at her top shelf. She was measuring what she had put by, what she had used, what she had left. In turn she looked at the small cupboard they had settled in one corner and each visit there was like going to the general store in town; it held much of her hopes for the time being. That was like saying it wouldn't last forever, or for the whole winter. She tried to avoid further thoughts on the matter.

But Prescott was gone and Christmas was coming to sit empty at her doorstep. Sadness hit her and she brushed it off immediately just the way she'd brush away a cobweb or a spider web that drifted down from an upper reach.

The doubts fell away when she recalled Prescott's smile. It was always a pleasant sight. Her gaze fell on the boys still buried in deep covers, probably measuring the temperature and how it would feel on them as they rose to get dressed. Each was smiling at her from their warm covers, their smiles more pleasant than Prescott's, like Gerard's, full of thanks as well as love.

Christmas without presents for them bothered her until she smelled the bread again, and gave thanks for its promise, and the aroma of venison with a burnt edge all of them liked pushed her into quick thanks for her husband's hunting skills and his dogged manner, even if it had brought them here to this place without presents for her children.

Gerard, she knew, never needed much more than her in his life. She gave thanks for that.

It was in that one thought, in that one minute, that she realized she had forgotten to mark off the last spent day. This was really a day later; this was really Christmas Day. Muriel Fiddler almost fainted. She had lost a day. This was Christmas Day. The boys, without saying a word, knew it. Gerard obviously knew it, and had not said a word about it.

She was crushed. The meal she was preparing they'd had for three days in a row. She had not prepared anything different, anything extra.

As she shook her head, she heard her two sons whispering under their covers. Were they talking about surprise Christmas presents? Was their mother playing a game with them, being so usual in her actions? Was Gerard saying little but thinking much?

She didn't know what to do. Best to continue her day, their day, the way she was going. What else could she do but be the mother of the brood? The mother in the apron, at the stove, at meal preparation, at the real important things in life.

"You two stay under the covers until I tell you to get dressed." Insistence was in her voice, and they did not move.

Spinning on one leg, the knife still in her hand, Gerard looking at her as if he had lost the day already, she said, "Might as well get some more of that wood in here, Gerard, while I have the stove nice and hot. Best bring in a couple of days' worth. We'll use it up. The stove's really hot. Best do it now."

She spun back to her work. The two boys sank deeper under covers because the section of wall would be taken down, wood drawn from the pile, the air coming in like a small blast from the far north.

Gerard Fiddler, dreamer, doer, believer in most things, especially in his wife and his children, thankful for at least one good friend and comrade in this life, hastened to do as bid by his wife.

The wall boards, fully vertical all the way, came loose when he took down the three cross bars that Prescott had put in place. He had done the trick once earlier, just to test it out. The task was easy, and he was thankful for it, thinking of the snow out there. He reached into the pile and extracted the cut logs one piece at a time, sometimes two at a time, his hands feeling the cold come on them with a thick and penetrating smoothness, but no snow coming in with the wood. He almost had a few days' worth piled on the side before he stacked them beside the stove, when his hand, in another reach into the pile, felt something softer than logs.

He withdrew his hand, then reached again, touched again, and made a sound of surprise in his throat that made Muriel jump, fearing he had been bitten by an incredible critter. The boys had come to sitting positions in their bed across the room, tossing off furs, old coats, and flour bags sewed into severe thickness, ready for whatever.

All of them, Gerard Fiddler, his wife Muriel and their two sons, were frozen in place as Christmas, long thought to be absent from this day, came into view as gaily wrapped packages, four of them, one after another, fell into the room at the feet of Gerard Fiddler. His wife looked on in absolute joy, his sons too, all of them realizing that Camden Prescott had done it again, remembered something else he had seen, some special happening that made Christmas the special day it was supposed to be, even as the wind whistled again atop them, winter with a full grip.

Muriel Fiddler had her wish come true and she was sure that Camden Prescott had wanted his wish to be found on Christmas Day, just the way he planned it.

Destination Idaho

Rockland Guidry, we should know up front, was never addressed from the time he was eight years old and a half year in school as Rockland. "Rocky" he was from his first encounter in a harsh world, and so they remained, Rocky his name and the harsh world around him. He'd never known a true home for any decent period in the early years and this place he was studying after a long ride looked as though it would prove to be the place to tie his horse, drop his hat and rest his bones ... for a spell, if not longer. He'd already decided he liked the taste of the air, how the sun warmed his back instead of burning it, how this place dipped its mysteries into secret valleys and canyons he might never visit, how a stream found its way again after a journey through lost and buried channels in the mountains as though the stream too had found its route and place.

Rocky Guidry rode out of Louisiana heading north for several weeks, found the view he was looking for on the side of a slow-rising hill above a clear, wide river in Idaho, noting the tall peaks in the distance, the steady flow of the river in late August, and off to the end of the valley, as if a chess master had set up a special board, the small spread dotted with a few barns or sheds, squares of three corrals, a north-running open-range pasture almost as big as the valley and a woman on horseback. She was just leaving the small main house. He saw this rider as the center piece of a magnificent setting and wondered how long it would take to meet her.

In his looking glass he made quick judgments, sure of his early assessments. The woman, riding with dash and class, obviously of the younger set, was headed south where the tops of a few buildings in a nearby town unknown to him caught the sun and reflected sheets of golden light at several edges. He thought them to be semaphores of special significance. Charm of a special magnitude comforted him, made the saddle softer, his legs unwearied, his eyes finding continual beauty in manifold objects between sky and good earth. In these past several days he had seen hawks and eagles and vultures sharing the high blue and the cross currents of winds, sheep on rocky ledges and cattle on verdant grass in quiet repose, wild horses and elk and buffalo sharing ground and grass, puma and wolf and coyote in their continual search of prey. His heart overflowed with the freedom and promise in all the Earth around him.

He wondered, in his pausing, if home was a place you found or a place you made for yourself. The answer could be right out in front of him.

In this pacific mood, he agreed that serenity and peace might have a chance in the area, a chance and a change that he deeply wanted, needed, implored of the high heavens. His immediate past was brittle to one who might have heard of him with a tainted ear, preset by many for strangers, new arrivals, possible contestants in the game of romance.

Rocky Guidry had been arrested for murder, charged, tried, sentenced to hang, all on the word of a careless drifter who had been fed a bag of beans and hot air by an enemy of Guidry. It had taken a gang of chain-ganged prisoners, laying low in the brush by order of their guard, who had seen the murder take place, committed by the man who had bought off the drifter, naming him as a witness.

When the gang of prisoners rode into the town on a wagon and saw the scaffold being erected and heard the story of the killing and the quick and efficient trial, the prisoners' guard asked the sheriff why the guilty man was walking around town as free as any of the spectators.

"What do you mean, Shavers?" the sheriff asked, for he had known the man on earlier meetings. "We have a witness that saw the whole damned thing."

He was about to walk away when Shavers replied, "And I got me nine men who saw that dude loafing around down there in front of the general store like he come into town to see a hanging and who's really the dude who shot that gent at the head of the bayou that you've pointed out as the murder scene."

"Nine men?" the sheriff said.

"No," replied Shavers. "Ten men, including me and my word will stand up to anything that dude can say, and you know it. Let's go down there and get this straightened out so you won't have the biggest faux pas hanging over you that you could ever try on for size, which looks mighty like it right now from where I'm standing, and those boys with me who'll shout to high heavens to say you, the sheriff, has been dead wrong in this, and won't that get a rise out of them folks so hoodwinked by a scoundrel, 'Dead wrong, aye.'?" He pronounced "dead wrong" as though it was right there in the uniformed chain of command.

Guidry, surprised at the quick turnaround, was let out of jail, fully pardoned and released with the profound apologies of the judge and the sheriff. He did not even stay to see the trial of the new defendant, saying, "I've had enough of my hometown for now."

Four weeks later he was in Colorado having passed through parts of Arkansas, Texas, Oklahoma, and Kansas. Idaho, for some unknown but compelling reason, had latched onto his interest and headed him there. He didn't know why but thought all along that Providence in some way was on his side and had not left him alone in the world. All that despite his harried days in jail and the quickness of the trial, everybody as anxious as Hell to get rid of him; and so they would be rid of him ... and as fast as he could make it out of town.

"I'm coming, Idaho," he'd said a hundred times under his breath or aloud as he rode along, seeing the land more than he'd ever seen it, and not once satisfied he was looking at his piece of Heaven here on Earth. And not once did he go over in his mind the cause and the circumstances of the murder, the trial, the accusation. What was done was over and he let it be, the words leaving him as he took in another totally free and delicious breath, this time on a stretch of green grass in Colorado and the peaks leaning over him, the magnificence of some scenes drawing hard at his determination to keep moving in his search.

For whatever reason presenting itself within a positive sense, Guidry believed the woman was leading him to where he wanted to go. "Ma'am," he said with heavy determination, "I sure hope to see you soon and make your acquaintance. It appears Heaven hasn't left me in the lurch anymore."

To his horse he said, "Let's go, Bayou Boy, and find the lady of our dreams." There was no hesitation on the part of Bayou Boy whose loping stride headed him toward the near town still tossing reflections of light as strong as signals.

Those signals would prove to be dangerous, complicit, suggestive and, with a good turn of luck, as providential and as comfortable as Guidry could possibly imagine; and the woman in the distance, the adept rider, would as believed from the first to be the center of it all. He realized any new place bore the mysteries that had created it, sent it on its way into history, and in the end become what it was meant to be.

The place was Torbick Falls, three dozen buildings of all sizes and all needs, sitting above the banks of the Three Silvers River. All of it, from some overheard discussion deep in his past, had drawn him here as though Fate had set it all in motion.

He was in Idaho and in Idaho he would stay. It wouldn't be easy, it would be easy to say, from the very first as he counted the conceived options; he was a stranger and such creatures were looked upon as suspicious, not at all above reproach, guilty of something somewhere or else why would they be here, unless they could prove themselves worthy of some accord.

Guidry could feel it in the air as he rode, the plusses and minuses coming at him like a rockfall on a runaway. The first stop, at The Bald Eagle Saloon, was not only the tip-off but the core of reception in the town towards strangers, first visitors, new faces. This was even before he had a chance to ask about the girl riding onto the town a few hours earlier on a bold-looking chestnut stallion, spirited, suitably paired with the attractive and adept rider, most likely the girl of his dreams come to town.

A small, wizened looking man, sparrow-thin in the face, his last meal perhaps a week in the past, his thirst heavier than hunger, who stood tight against the bar at seeing Guidry, let his voice roar with pointed curiosity, when he asked the bartender, 'Shaver, you know that gent just walked in like we said hello come on in, when we didn't? Well, I saw his picture in a paper in Kansas. He was let loose of a killin' down in bayou country and appears to have run away from it, right or wrong, all the way up here with us hardy folks who don't like killers of the southern sort, which sure is bayou country with more boats than horses hangin' about. Can you believe any and all of that, like it's a whole lot of queer stuff for us to swaller?"

"Whisperin'," the bartender said, "you sure ain't whisperin' none now." The bar rag in his hand went sweeping across the bar top as though he was erasing all traces of the conversation just made public. It also said he realized his livelihood depended on social drinkers, thirsty cowboys and god-awful drunks letting go of themselves ... which happened too often when Whisperin' was around, which was too often for one man.

Guidry was sure it was the biggest mouthful of nothing the thin-faced gent had uttered in a month of talking. Plus, the speaker was trying all sorts of gestures to add voice and intention to his words as he shook his shoulders, hunched one of them towards Guidry as sharp as a pointed finger, and nodded at his own piece of affirmation, even as he put himself forward as disheveled, unkempt and outright sore on the eyes.

Guidry was sure the mouthy one didn't want to get into a fight, but sure would like to see one develop, so he stepped towards him and said, "You seem to know a lot of what's going on around here. Do you know the name of the girl riding a bold-looking chestnut stallion that came into town a few hours ago from north of here? Both her and her horse kind of high-spirited and pretty as good sunrises."

"Her name's Marsha-Thistle Lee and there's gents already havin' interest in her, local gents, if you get my drift, gents proper to the town and not southern runaways of a new kind, if you get my drift there too."

"Well, I'm sure glad, Whisperin', that you're not running any kind of Welcome Wagon for Torbick Falls or the place would fall flat on its face before you could shake a hand with a stranger. But I'll be sure to tell Miss Marsha-Thistle Lee that you were the gent who provided me with her name and where she lives."

Whisperin' jumped at that and said, "I didn't say one word about the Cross Bar Spread," and tried to shut his mouth and most likely bit his tongue at the muted attempt, too late for silence and busy-bodying.

Behind the bar, Shaver was his usual self at any hint of humor, as he started shaking his whole frame in concert with the conversation in front of him, and he looked up with another interest as a good looking gent packing two good looking pistols on his belt entered The Bald Eagle Saloon.

The man was as clean and natty in his trail duds as Whisperin' was dirty, his eyes reacting to the inner dimness of the room in contrast with some obvious days on a sun-baked trail. Well-fit in the body, wide-shouldered, looking to be in his 40s and handsome in a rugged way, he nodded at Guidry, at Shaver behind the bar and ignored Whisperin' as if he had enough of him long before this moment.

Guidry caught the distance and dislike immediately, and decided he liked the man's attitude on the spot, and liked him further when he extended his hand and said, "Well, you're a stranger here and if Whisperin' didn't welcome you in a proper manner, I will. I'm Dan Hurley, just in from delivering a herd to the army downriver at Fort Gibson. I'm thirsty, hungry for any outside news I haven't heard, and glad to see a new face in an old town that some days chokes on itself."

Whisperin' leaped in to the conversation by blurting out, "He made me tell him Miss Marsha's name and where she lives. Damned first thing he did comin' in here." One hand was on his hip and the other hand had not yet found the other hip, as though the hand had no sense of feel in it.

Shaver was still shaking.

Hurley, easy on words, easy on emotion, said, "Well, that girl cooks a great meal, rides like a damned fool cowboy on show-off day, is the best looker of all the gals around here, and I'm one of the gents interested in her, with no promises and no great hopes as yet. But I don't get excited. I've been married, have two kids, lost my wife to some bad infection a couple of years ago, and my time is mostly business time."

His handshake with Guidry was authentic as well as warm.

Picking up the tone where Hurley left off, Guidry said, "My name's Rocky Guidry, freed from prison down in Louisiana just before I was supposed to get hung for something I didn't do and dreamed about Idaho all the time I was in jail and wanted out of Louisiana. I saw the lady in question from high in the hills and she made a great introduction to Idaho. I dare say I'd love to meet her, but Whisperin' here thinks it's against the local law, or something like that. Saw my picture in a paper in Kansas that was celebrating justice on my part and twisted the tale to suit his mouth."

It was Hurley's time to shake and laugh and he said, "You hit him on the head of the nail, right on. If you're looking for work, I'll be hiring soon, but so's Marsha's dad at the Cross Bar Spread just north of here.

He's a great gent, widowed like me as his wife was killed by some unknown bad ass with a wild gun. He's looking for a woman like me, and unlucky like me so far."

Rocky Guidry smiled, nodded, and said, "I just knew that Idaho was going to be home for me, a new home. I like the start."

Getting his horse taken care of, Guidry snagged a place to sleep in the mow, slept deep and rose early, had a diner breakfast with two other early risers, and saddled up Bayou Boy for an early ride up the river, heading for the Cross Bar spread.

The land was gorgeous in all aspects as he rode, the grass green, animals active in many sections (he noted sheep, bison and a few wild horses, all quite different from Louisiana and could have lauded the changes), the rocks and hills off to the northeast capped with a few white peaks saying winter would be interesting, and sat his saddle with comfort.

When he saw the sudden quick reflection from high in a rocky formation, he dove from the saddle as a bullet whined over his head. He fired his pistol into the ground and Bayou Boy sprinted across the grass until he went out of sight in a copse of trees.

He remained motionless, though his eyes scanned the area where the shot came from. He saw nothing move but animals on a lower level, making him think eventually that the shooter had moved on. When a bird of prey came down like a thunderbolt and grabbed off some squirming critter from the grass, Guidry rolled himself into a swale in high grass, slipped deeper into the grass, and finally moved into the shade of a small group of trees.

No shots followed him. When he whistled, Bayou Boy was at his side. The pair went looking through the higher area where the shot had come from. Guidry would tell a few folks later on that it was Bayou Boy's quick reaction to a reflection that led him to a discharged shell on a shelf of rock. From his inspection of the casing he determined it was newly fired, the smell of burnt powder still alive no weather had hit it yet. He didn't know what it was, but he'd find someone who'd identify it for him.

He put the shell casing in his pocket and rode on to the Cross Bar spread.

He saw her when he topped a small rise as she hauled water up from a well and emptied the bucket in a trough. Four horses surrounded her as they drank and he saw little more of her until a man called to her from the wide porch and said, "Company's coming."

She took one look at him and sprinted to the house, the man on the porch raising his hands in full expectation of the move, and waved Guidry on to the porch. "That was my daughter Marsha doing the dash," he said. "Does it every time a young, good-looking man comes to visit. She'll be out in a bit. I'm Jed Lee and this is my spread, the Cross Bar. My daughter's name is Marsha-Thistle Lee and she's much like her mother was; a spark for a man. I was lucky, but lost her to an accident."

"I'm Rocky Guidry, once of Louisiana, now of Idaho, and looking for work. Dan Hurley said you might be looking for good help."

Lee laughed. "He's looking too. Now there's a good man for you." He shook his head in wonder, and Guidry read his mind perfectly.

Before he could produce the shell and ask for its identification, Marsha-Thistle Lee came out of the house and Guidry stared open-mouthed at her beauty. Both her and her father noted the expression on the Louisianan's face.

"Mr. Rocky Guidry, this is my daughter, Marsha-Thistle Lee, 21, unmarried, rider, roper, cook, and too much like her mother to allow me too much comfort." His smile was a saddle wide.

The young ones shook hands, her eyes aglow with new interest, his too, and in the middle of a thought, Mr. Lee said, "He's looking for work," and she said, in a sudden burst, "He's hired."

They talked a while, had lunch on the porch and she gave him a quick tour of the ranch, part of it on horseback, part of it on foot.

Guidry was in love, had felt all along that life in Idaho would prove highly interesting, and was about to depart the house when he remembered the shell casing in his pocket and said to the elder Lee, "Can you tell me what kind of a shell this is? I saw its reflection on the trail, that's how I found it."

Marsha grabbed it from his hand with a loud and surprising exclamation, "Pa, it looks like it would fit the Sharps up there on the wall." She pointed to a rifle hanging over the fireplace.

"It sure is, Marsha. It's a .50 caliber cartridge for a rifle just like this Sharps of mine, an 1874 model that caught a round directly into its innards the first time I was ever going to use it, out there after a wolf had fed on about enough of my herd. Saved my life, it did, when it caught that wild round from some wild man out there." He shook his head in wonder and looked sheepishly at his daughter. "Thought I'd hang it up there for looks. It's proven to be a topic of conversation whenever we have company." He tipped his head at Guidry. "You're not familiar with rifles?"

"Never fired one of them, that's for sure. Looks like a lot of gun. Many of them around? Is it a long range weapon?"

"About one of the best," Lee answered. "There are a few of them around. Mountain men are favored of them, for game mostly when hunger strikes them. I won this one in a poker game when I caught a pair of aces for a full house, but never got to fire it." He was sheepish again.

"It's okay, Pa," she replied, "I know. I wish Mom had one in her hands when she was hit. That was all of ten years ago, but it's still strange to me." There was a small thrust of her chin, as if a secret vow had been touched anew.

There were secrets here, Guidry thought, whose inside stories he had to know.

But Guidry, not saying much else except for his goodbye and promise to be back with his gear in a day or two, had the answer he was looking for ... or part way to revelation he figured. The image of the Sharps was cemented in his mind along with other images that began to filter through his mind, and when he rode off he was filled with those sudden images and the constant beauty of Marsha-Thistle Lee, a woman with the looks found on no woman he had ever seen. She had released something in her besides beauty during his visit, and he plumbed the depths of his being, hoping to read things the right way, that she had a real interest in him. Aiding him, of course, was her hurried, and decidedly affirmative words, "He's hired." He kept hearing her voice saying the words, trying to put the nicest tone in the works of them. She spoke fast, rode fast, decided fast, and he shoved his mind to slow things down to a solid, pleasant, long-lasting otherwise, dream-wise trip back to Torbick Falls.

The uneasy idea of getting closer to her rode with him all the way.

He went directly to the saloon and met Dan Hurley on the way in. "How'd you make out at the Lee spread?"

"I've been hired." he said it with a wide smile on his face.

"C'mon, I'll buy you lunch and you can handle the beer. Deal?"

"Sure is, and there's something I'd like to talk to you about."

Hurley, of course, assumed it was about Marsha right from the outset. But he was wrong.

They had been served a beer and a thick sandwich, after which Guidry looked around the room and slid the shell casing across the table, keeping it out of sight, and asked, "Many guns around here fit this?"

Hurley, understanding Guidry's body language and his attempt at secrecy, looked quizzical, but said in quick response, "It comes from a Sharps, probably 1874, but I don't have one. Was this meant for you?" He kept it in the palm of his right hand, as though he had to squeeze it out of sight. "It leads me to think it was and that you and the Lees had a talk about it and you're now a one-man search party."

He patted Guidry on the back. "You need any help, just ask. I have had some strange questions in my mind over the years, so I'm offering help right up front, just trying to get answers also." His voice, its tone and its words, were past doubt, thus were authentic in Guidry's mind.

Rocky Guidry had an ally he could count on, so continued with a plan of sorts. 'I'm looking for one man, who fired at me in the hills while I was going out to the Lee's spread. Mr. Lee showed me his shot-up Sharps rifle, and I went off and running. They hired me on as a hand, but I'll look for the bushwhacker forever if I have to. I know I can't track all over Hell and Creation to catch him, but I can try to keep my eyes on any man who totes one of these Sharps 1874 in his arsenal. I'll have to use the town as a backdrop along with occasional encounters on the trail for men carrying a Sharps 1874. If you'll keep watch in town, I'd sure appreciate it. Just a list of names will do. I'll do the smoking out. No sense you getting caught up in my deep interests and someone else's cross hairs. I'll make sure anything needed in town by the Lees comes to my chasing down. That'll ease your burden."

The new alliance parted ways after another round of beer.

And so it was that any errand calling for a visit to town, it was Rocky Guidry who made himself most quickly available. He'd jump on Bayou Boy and be on his way.

And it happened so many times, and so quickly, that Lee and his daughter talked about it, the father saying to her, "It might mean he has a 'friend' in town he'd like to see as often as possible. You have to face that, Marsha." It was the way he said it that did not find favor with her. It cut to the quick and she fired back, "His eyes can't lie to me, Pa. I know that. I knew that from the first minute. It's just the way Ma said it, that you could never lie to her."

And so it was that almost four months later, a list of four men, not including Lee, each sported a Sharps 1874 in their saddle sheath. The list came from observation in and about the saloon and the general store, where ammunition was sold, and the livery, and from casual conversations in the saloon about marksmanship and rifle toting in general.

Of the four Sharps carriers, two seemed entirely free of any suspicion ... to a point. And the other two seemed so loaded with suspicion and a kind of tempered hatred for different objects or objections, like fences, landowners and sassy, saucy daughters of the same landowners that they deserved and got closer inspection from the alliance; Lee being one of the landowners did not appear to count.

Both men of the new alliance promised they'd keep their eyes open for any shortfall of information or dastardly trends concerning any of the suspects ... at the saloon, the store, the livery or possible encounters on all trails beyond town.

Guidry, on good days, like Saturday or Sunday, a week's work under his belt, took to sitting out front of the Bald Eagle Saloon, hat tipped on his head, seat tipped under him, but his eyes on all saddle sheaths for Sharps 1874's as horses were hitched at the rail in front of him.

The first man on the third Saturday of August was Hatchet Jack Hubbard, a burly mountain man, wide as an ox, thick as an oak trunk, mean as a cornered bore or a rattler, whose horse looked too tired to carry him and arrived thirsty. Dirt and grime beat on him, meaning the rider had not visited the river on his way to town but was waiting to get a drink first. The mount looked as though he needed a drink more than Hatchet Jack, road and trail dust in a frothy mix on his frame.

Guidry, having seen him in the saloon before, said, "Morning, Hatchet Jack, you get a glimmer of that big bear up on the trail everybody's been talking about? Think you could knock him down with that gun of yours? Some of the boys say he's a real big one, terror of the hills some say." His hat was still tipped as was his chair.

Hatchet Jack Hubbard apparently didn't like Guidry right from the start of his arrival as a stranger in town but came back with hard retort, "With that rifle I can knock down anything I see in a thousand yards or even better. Don't stand no chance with me. I never miss."

Guidry snapped to attention, rose from his seat, flipped his hat back on his head and dug in his vest pocket.

Holding out the shell casing, the sun catching it just the same way he saw it the first time, and said, "Did you miss with this one?"

The shell casing glittered in his hand, the sun bouncing away from it like a cosmic shot.

Hubbard was alive with anger. "I never miss. Never. This is the best gun ever. I never miss. Where'd you get that shell?"

"Found it on a bushwhacker's ledge high in the hills after a round just missed me. Just missed me." He held his fingers about an inch apart. "Missed me by that much." He shook his head in disgust at the shooting result.

"You think I shot at you from cover?" I ought to call you out on that. You better go get a gun and put it on, then I'll call you out." Puffing himself up, thrusting his chest out, he appeared bigger than ever, double the threat he was, death in his hands one way or another.

Guidry was totally cool at the sight and at the threat. "What difference does wearing a gun make? I wasn't wearing a gun when the round from this shell missed me by a whole inch. He held his fingers even wider apart, exaggerating the miss. "You really that good or that bad?"

Flushed, angered all to Hell and back, Hubbard, screamed, "You're a snotty-assed kid too good for folks. Been that way since you come high-falootin' in here and got a job out at the Lee's place. Nobody 'round here wants you around, like we heard you was a killer down there in swamp country." The disdain and hatred rode his face deep as a mine shaft. "They was talkin' 'bout you 'fore you got here. That's got a lot of meanin' in it."

Rocky Guidry was primed. "Does that mean you have something else in mind? I don't carry a gun." He showed his empty waistline; no gun belt, no holster, no side arm.

Hubbard walked to his horse, pulled the Sharps from the sheath, and as he turned, to face Guidry, he unfastened his gun belt and heaved it, holster, pistol and all, to Guidry, who caught it in flight as a reaction.

"You're armed now, Swamp Boy."

He was about to raise the Sharps when a solid, loud, clear click of a gun sounded and the two adversaries turned to face Ben Hurley at the head of alley alongside the saloon holding two pistols directly on Hubbard. He said, "Drop that gun belt, Rocky. I've got him covered."

Guidry carefully sat the gun belt on the boardwalk as the sheriff came on the scene, saying, "I heard your whole confession, Hubbard. Shooting at this stranger and killing Mrs. Annabelle Lee all that long ago."

"I never said that. It was an accident," Hubbard yelled loudly in a defensive voice, and stiffened as if he finally understood what he had said, all of which most of Torbick Falls heard also, the long mystery solved.

Over drinks in the saloon, Hurley said, "I was thinking of making a trip out to see Marsha on my own account, unless you got that territory all wrapped up."

"I never talk about women like that," Guidry said, with not a single smile in the works, not a one, but seeing images that Hurley would never see. Somehow Hurley already knew his time was beaten, from Guidry's silent expression.

About the Author

Thomas F. Sheehan served in the 31st Infantry, Korea, 1951-52, and graduated Boston College, 1956. Books include *Epic Cures; Brief Cases, Short Spans; The Saugus Book; This Rare Earth & Other Flights; Ah, Devon Unbowed; Reflections from Vinegar Hill.* eBooks include *Korean Echoes (nominated for a Distinguished Military Award)*, *The Westering*, (nominated for National Book Award); from *Danse Macabre* are *Murder at the Forum, Death of a Lottery Foe, Death by Punishment, An Accountable Death and Vigilantes East. A Collection of Friends, From the Quickening, In the Garden of Long Shadows, The Nations, Where Skies Grow Wide, Cross Trails, The Cowboys,* and *Beside the Broken Trail* were published by Pocol Press, and *Six Guns, Inc.*, by *Nazar Look*, in Romania. Sheehan has multiple works at these sites: *Rosebud, Linnet's Wings, Serving House Journal, Copperfield Review, KYSO Flash, La Joie Magazine, Soundings East, Literary Orphans, Indiana Voices Journal, Frontier Tales, Western Online Magazine, Provo Canyon Review, Nazar Look, Eastlit, Rope & Wire Magazine, Ocean Magazine, The Literary Yard, Green Silk Journal, Fiction on the Web, The Path, Faith-Hope and Fiction, The Cenacle,* etc. Sheehan's tales have produced 30 Pushcart nominations, and five Best of the Net nominations (and one winner) and short story awards from *Nazar Look* for 2012-2015. *Swan River Daisy* was recently released by KY Stories and *Back Home in Saugus*, 200 pages, 90,000 words, and a chapbook, *Small Victories for the Soul*, are on proposal. (His Amazon Author's Page, Tom Sheehan -- is on the Amazon site.)

Made in the USA
Columbia, SC
01 July 2018